THE SISTERS GRIMM

BOOK FOUR

ONCE UPON A CRIME

Other books in the *Sisters Grimm* series

THE SISTERS GRIMM

BOOK FOUR

ONCE UPON A CRIME

MICHAEL BUCKLEY

pictures by Peter Ferguson

Amulet Books
New York

Library of Congress Cataloging-in-Publication Data:
Buckley, Michael.
The sisters Grimm, book four : once upon a crime / Michael Buckley ;
pictures by Peter Ferguson.
p. cm.
Summary: When the fairy-tale detectives rush to New York City hoping to find an
Everafter who can cure Puck, they trigger a chain of events that includes a murder
mystery, and learn many new things about their mother who, along with their father,
is still in an enchanted sleep.
ISBN-13: 978-0-8109-1610-4 (clothbound, embossed)
ISBN-10: 0-8109-1610-X (clothbound, embossed)
[1. Characters in literature—Fiction. 2. Sisters—Fiction. 3. Grandmothers—Fiction.
4. New York (N.Y.)—Fiction. 5. Mystery and detective stories.]
I. Ferguson, Peter, 1968– ill. II. Title. III. Title: Once upon a crime.
PZ7.B882323Siw 2007
[Fic]—dc22
2006033516

Printed and bound in U.S.A.
10 9 8 7 6 5 4 3 2 1

HNA ▌▌▌▌▌
harry n. abrams, inc.
a subsidiary of La Martinière Groupe

115 West 18th Street
New York, NY 10011
www.hnabooks.com

For my mother, Wilma Cuvelier

ACKNOWLEDGMENTS

It seems as though the more of these books I write the more people I have to thank. I hope you all know how invaluable you have been.

First and foremost, thanks to my editor, Susan Van Metre, for her inexhaustible patience and insight. I also want to thank everyone at Abrams Books, most notably Jason Wells, for their support, hard work, and cheerleading. My wife, Alison, deserves special praise, not only for her efforts as my literary agent, but also for being the greatest thing that has ever happened to me. As always, a special thanks to Joe Deasy for his praise, criticism, and hilariously inappropriate humor. I also send out special thanks to Molly Choi, Maureen Falvey, David Snidero, and Susan Holtz-Minihane for friendship that goes above and beyond the call of duty. And to the members of Team Buckley at Wall Intermediate: Lauren, Jillian, Amanda, Meghan, Tim, Dana, Kim, Katherine, Jack, and Veronica.

Lastly, thanks to Daisy, who passed away during the writing of this book. Daisy was a West Highland White Terrier my wife found in the Czech Republic eleven years ago. Daisy was probably my single biggest inspiration. I'll miss her playfulness and sweet nature. I hope the squirrels are fast in heaven because here she comes.

THE SISTERS GRIMM

BOOK FOUR

ONCE UPON A CRIME

"GET OFF THE STREETS!" SABRINA CRIED. *"There's a monster coming!"*

"Do you people want to get squashed?" Daphne shouted, but the pedestrians were used to ignoring screaming lunatics. Daphne turned to Granny Relda with a panicked face. *"They won't listen!"*

Granny Relda took the girls by the hand. *"They will. Run, children!"*

The girls shared a nervous glance as they raced down the sidewalk, pushing through the crowd and calling out warnings to anyone who would listen. As far as Sabrina knew, her grandmother had never run from anything. She was the bravest woman Sabrina and her sister had ever met. Soon, the family came to an intersection and stopped in their tracks. They weren't on the quiet streets of Ferryport Landing anymore; this was the big city. If they tried to cross against the light, a truck or a speeding taxi would flatten them. While they waited anxiously, Sabrina took a quick look back, in time to see the entire front of the building they had just been standing in collapse. A huge leg stepped through the rubble. The people around them paused, then let out a collective scream.

"They're paying attention now," Sabrina muttered.

With a dreadful pounding, the gigantic creature freed itself of the store. Its lantern eye scanned the streets far below and fixed on Sabrina.

"I'll get you, my pretty," the monster cried, then lifted one of its enormous, pointed shoes and kicked a taxicab out of the way, sending it slamming into a light pole and then skidding into the intersection, where it crashed into a newspaper delivery truck.

A wave of terror rolled through the crowded street; pedestrians turned as one mass and rushed toward Sabrina and her family. Many people were looking back as they ran; a young woman knocked Daphne to the ground in her panic. If the monster didn't kill the Grimms, Sabrina realized, they would be trampled to death by the mob.

1

The explosion shook Sabrina Grimm so hard she swore she felt her brain do a somersault inside her skull. As she struggled to get her bearings, a noxious, black smoke choked her, burning her eyes. Could she escape? No, she was at the mercy of the cold, soulless machine otherwise known as the family car.

"Isn't anyone worried that this hunk of junk might kill us?" she cried, but no one heard her over the chaos.

As usual, Sabrina was the only person in her family who noticed anything was wrong. Murder plots, horrifying monsters, the shaking, jostling, rattling death trap the Grimms called transportation: Sabrina had her eyes wide open to trouble.

She was sure if she didn't stay on her toes her entire family would be dead by nightfall. They were lucky to have her.

Her grandmother, a kind, sweet old lady, was in the front seat, buried in the book she had been reading for the last two hours. Next to her was the old woman's constant companion, a skinny, grouchy old man named Mr. Canis, who drove the family everywhere. Sharing the backseat with Sabrina was a portly, pink-skinned fellow named Mr. Hamstead, and nestled between them was Daphne, Sabrina's seven-year-old sister, who had been slumbering peacefully the entire ride, drooling like a faucet onto Sabrina's coat sleeve. Sabrina gently nudged her sister toward Mr. Hamstead. He grimaced when he noticed the drool and shot Sabrina a look that said, *Thanks for nothing.*

Sabrina pretended not to notice and leaned forward to get her grandmother's attention. Granny Relda set her book down in her lap and turned to Sabrina with smiling eyes. The old woman's face was etched in wrinkles, but her pink cheeks and button nose gave her a youthful appearance. She always wore colorful dresses and matching hats with a sunflower appliqué in the center. Today she was in purple.

"Where are we?" Sabrina shouted.

Her grandmother cupped a hand to her ear to let Sabrina know she hadn't heard the question over the car's terrific racket.

"Are we getting close to Faerie yet?"

"Oh, I love chili, but I'm afraid it doesn't love me," Granny shouted back.

"No, not chili! Faerie!" Sabrina cried. "Are we getting close?"

"Why no, I've never kissed a monkey. What a weird question."

Sabrina was about to throw up her hands in defeat when Mr. Canis turned to her. "We are not far," he barked and turned his gaze back to the road. The old man had better hearing than anyone.

Sabrina sighed with relief. All of the rumbling and sputtering would soon be over, and it would all have been worth it to help Puck. She looked at the shivering boy huddled next to her grandmother. His blond hair was matted to his head and his face was drenched in sweat. Sabrina felt a pang of guilt in her belly. If it weren't for her they wouldn't be on this trip at all.

She sat back in her seat as the car came to a stop at a cross-roads. She looked out the window. To the left was farmland as far as she could see. To the right a dusty country road leading to a tiny, distant house. Behind her was Ferryport Landing, her new hometown, and ahead . . . she wasn't sure. A place called Faerie, her grandmother had said. They were taking Puck home.

As the car rolled forward, Sabrina lost herself in memories. It seemed like a lifetime ago when she had had a home. Once she'd been a normal kid living on the Upper East Side of New York City, with a mom and a dad, a baby sister, and an apartment near the park. Life had been simple and easy and ordinary. Then one day her parents, Henry and Veronica, disappeared. The police looked for them but all they found was their abandoned car and a single clue—a red handprint left on the dashboard.

With no one to take care of the girls, Sabrina and Daphne were dumped into an orphanage and assigned to Minerva Smirt, an ill-tempered caseworker who hated children. She'd taken a special dislike to the Grimm sisters and for almost a year and a half had stuck them with foster families who used and abused them. These so-called loving caregivers forced the girls to be their personal maids, pool cleaners, and ditch diggers. More often than not, the families were in it for the state check. Some were just plain crazy.

When Granny Relda took in the sisters, Sabrina was sure the old woman was one of the crazies. First, their grandmother was *supposed* to be dead. Second, Relda moved the girls to a little town on the Hudson River called Ferryport Landing, miles from civilization. Third, and most astounding, was that she claimed that her neighbors were all fairy-tale characters. Granny

Relda was convinced that the mayor was Prince Charming, the Three Little Pigs ran the police department, witches served pancakes at the diner, and ogres delivered the mail. She also claimed that Sabrina and Daphne were the last living descendants of Jacob and Wilhelm, the Brothers Grimm, whose book of fairy tales wasn't fiction but an account of actual events and the beginning of a record kept by each new generation of the family. Granny said it was the Grimm legacy to investigate any unusual crimes and to keep an eye on the mischief-making fairy-tale folk, also known as Everafters. In a nutshell, the girls were the next in a long line of "fairy-tale detectives."

After hearing Granny Relda's wild tale, Sabrina was sure her "grandmother" had forgotten to take her medication—that is, until a giant came along and kidnapped the old woman. Suddenly, her stories held a lot more weight.

After the sisters Grimm rescued their grandmother, they agreed to become fairy-tale detectives—Daphne enthusiastically, Sabrina reluctantly—and plunged headfirst into investigating the other freaky felonies of their new hometown.

Daphne loved every minute of their new lives. What seven-year-old wouldn't want to live in a town filled with bedtime stories come to life? But Sabrina couldn't get used to the strange people they encountered. She also distrusted the Everafters, and it was no secret that the community felt the same way about her family. Most thought the Grimms were meddlers. Others just downright despised them. Sabrina really couldn't blame them. After all, the Everafters were trapped in Ferryport Landing and it was her family's fault. Two hundred years prior, Wilhelm Grimm had constructed a magical barrier around the town in an effort to quell an Everafter rebellion against their human neighbors. And since then, the Everafters, whether good or bad, had been prisoners, and the Grimms, many felt, had been their prison guards.

But the real reason Sabrina didn't trust the Everafters was the red handprint the police had discovered on her missing parents' car. It was the mark of a secret Everafter organization called "the Scarlet Hand." No one knew who its members were, or the identity of the mysterious Master who was its leader.

A recent confrontation with Red Riding Hood, an agent of the Scarlet Hand, had led to the recovery of Sabrina and Daphne's missing parents. Unfortunately, Henry and Veronica were under a sleeping spell that the family didn't know how to break.

Puck, a family friend, had been injured helping the Grimm sisters fight the demented Red Riding Hood and her ferocious pet, the Jabberwocky. The monster had ripped off Puck's fairy wings, and now he was dangerously ill. Luckily for Puck, the Vorpal blade, which the Grimms had used to kill the Jabberwocky, could cut through anything, including the magical barrier around Ferryport Landing. Leaving Henry and Veronica in safe-keeping, Sabrina, Daphne, Granny Relda, and their trusted friends had set out with the sick boy, using the Vorpal blade to cut a hole big enough for the family car to drive through. Now they were on their way to Faerie, home of Puck's family, whom they hoped could make the young fairy well again.

Sabrina sighed, shifted in her seat, and wondered for the hundredth time when they'd get to Faerie. Then out of the corner of her eye she spotted blue-and-red lights flashing in the window behind them. Mr. Canis pulled the car over to the side of the road and turned off the engine.

"What's going on?" Sabrina asked.

"We're being pulled over by the police," Granny said. She and Mr. Canis shared a concerned look.

There was a tap on Mr. Canis's window. The old man rolled it down and a very angry police officer, wearing a short navy blue coat and sunglasses, peeked inside. He eyed the family suspiciously.

"Do you know why I pulled you over?" he said.

"Were we speeding?" Mr. Canis asked.

"Oh, I didn't pull you over for speeding. I pulled you over

because this . . . this tank you're driving is violating at least a hundred different environmental and safety laws. Let me see your driver's license."

Mr. Canis glanced at Granny Relda and then turned back to the policeman. "I'm afraid I don't have one."

The policeman laughed, seemingly in disbelief. "You've got to be kidding me. OK, folks, everyone step out of the car."

"Officer, I'm sure we can—"

The officer bent down. His smile was gone. "Step out of the car."

Granny turned in her seat to look at the girls and Mr. Hamstead. "OK, let's get out of the car."

Daphne was still sound asleep, so Sabrina shook her until the little girl opened her eyes.

"Whazzabigidea?" Daphne grumbled.

"Get up, we're going to jail," Sabrina said, helping her out of the car.

They were parked on a bridge and the wind coming off the water below was brutal. The cold air froze Sabrina to the bone as she watched cars and trucks whiz by. It was a terrible day, and the dark clouds hanging in the sky warned that it was going to get worse.

"Officer, if I could be of any assistance," Mr. Hamstead said as he tugged his pants up over his belly. "I happen to be the former sheriff of Ferryport Landing and—"

"Where?"

"Ferryport Landing. It's about two hours north."

"Well, as a former sheriff you should know it's against the law to ride around with someone who doesn't have a driver's license, let alone someone who is driving around in this menace." The policeman poked his head back into the car and spotted Puck. "Who's the kid?"

"He's my grandson and he's not feeling very well. We're taking him to a doctor," Granny said.

"Not in this thing, lady," the policeman said. "I'm impounding this vehicle for the good of humanity. I'll call an ambulance and have him taken to Columbia-Presbyterian Hospital."

He reached down to the walkie-talkie strapped to his waist and brought the device to his mouth. He barked an order for a tow truck as he watched the family suspiciously.

"If Puck is sent to a hospital, they're going to discover he's not human," Mr. Hamstead mumbled to Granny Relda.

"The boy needs a special kind of doctor," Canis growled to the cop.

"And the devil needs a glass of ice water," the officer snapped back. "You should be worrying about yourself. You're going to be lucky if you don't spend the night in jail. Does anyone have any identification?"

"Of course," Granny Relda said as she reached into her handbag. "I know I have my ID in here somewhere."

But the police officer was now focused on Mr. Canis. A big brown tail had slipped out of the back of the old man's pants and was blowing in the wind. The cop studied it for a moment, unsure of what it was, and then walked around Mr. Canis to get a better look.

"Is this a tail, buddy?" the policeman asked.

Sabrina looked anxiously at the old man, who was sweating in the icy air. His expression was nervous and angry. She'd been seeing this expression more and more lately. It was the look he got when the transformation came over him.

"Stay calm," Sabrina urged Mr. Canis, but he didn't seem to hear her. The change had already begun. Canis's nose morphed into a hairy snout and fur grew on his neck and hands. His body expanded, filling out the oversized suit he always wore. Black talons sprang from the tips of his fingers. Fangs crept down from his upper jaw. He was changing into his true form—that of the Big Bad Wolf, the carefully suppressed beast everyone feared would someday come out and never go back in.

The cop stood bewildered for a moment, then reached for his weapon.

"Oh, here it is," Granny said. She pulled her hand from inside her purse, opened her fist, and blew a puff of pink dust at the police officer. He froze, looking a bit befuddled, and then his eyes went glassy.

"You know, some days, being a policeman can be downright boring," Granny said.

"You're telling me," the officer said in a sleepy voice.

"Why, you didn't hand out a single speeding ticket today."

"Yeah, today was real dull."

"Now, get back into your car and have a great afternoon," Granny said.

"Will do," the officer said, obeying. Moments later he hopped into his squad car and drove away.

"Lucky I brought the forgetful dust," Granny said. She rested her hand on Mr. Canis's shoulder and immediately the transformation stopped, then slowly reversed. The old man shrank back to his human state.

"Relda, I am sorry," he said. "It has been a struggle as of late. Any little thing seems to set it off."

"No harm done," the old woman said. "But for the rest of this trip I suggest you hide your tail."

The old man nodded and did his best to tuck it into the back of his trousers.

"Wait a minute!" Sabrina cried as she watched the squad car drive away. On the back, painted in bright white letters, was NYPD. "That guy was a New York City cop!"

"Well, of course he was," Granny said as she pointed beyond the side of the bridge. Off on the horizon massive buildings reached upward along the skyline, as if competing for heaven's attention. Airplanes and helicopters flew above them. It was a scene Sabrina had witnessed many times before and her throat tightened as she fought back happy tears.

Daphne squinted out at the sparkling metropolis. One building stood taller than all the rest, tapering at the top into a fine silver point. She grabbed her older sister's arm and pointed at it.

"That's the Empire State Building!" she cried, quickly placing the palm of her hand into her mouth and biting down on it. It was one of Daphne's many quirks—the one that signaled that she was happy and excited.

"We're home!" Sabrina shouted back. "We're in New York City!"

The girls jumped up and down, chanting the sentence over and over again, louder and louder.

"Well, I'll be," Mr. Hamstead said as he approached the bridge railing. Pants were always a problem for the big-bellied gentleman, and he tugged on his now until they were hoisted back over his gut. Satisfied, he leaned on the railing and soaked in the view. The girls noticed his eyes well with tears.

Daphne rushed to his side and wrapped him up in a hug. "Don't cry, Mr. Hamstead. You'll make me cry."

"They're happy tears, Daphne," he said. "I never thought I'd see this place. I've been trapped in Ferryport Landing for a long time."

"You're going to love it! The city is the best! There is so much to do and see and eat! Oh, I can almost smell the hot dogs from here."

"Hot dogs!" Hamstead cried as his nose morphed into a runny, pink snout. Hamstead rarely slipped out of his human form, but when he got very excited his true identity as one of the Three Little Pigs was revealed.

"What did I say?" Daphne whispered to Sabrina.

"Hot dogs are made from pigs," Sabrina whispered back.

Daphne cringed. "I mean, uh, I would never, uh, eat a hot dog, you know . . . they're . . . uh, gross. What I meant to say was pepperoni pizza!"

The little girl looked at Sabrina for reassurance, but Sabrina could not give it to her. "Pepperoni, too."

"It is?"

Sabrina nodded.

Daphne cringed, again. "I mean broccoli. I can't wait to get a big piece to chew on. There's nothing like walking around the city with a big ol' head of broccoli."

"Oh yeah, New York is famous for its broccoli," Sabrina said.

Daphne stuck her tongue out at her sister.

"Wolf, you should see this!" Hamstead said, shaking off the girls' culinary suggestions. Mr. Canis joined him at the rail and gazed out at the marvelous city.

"Look at what we've missed," Hamstead whispered.

Canis leaned forward in wonder.

The two men stood in silence. The significance of the moment became clear to Sabrina. The whole world had kept on spinning while the Everafters were stuck in Ferryport Landing. Cities had risen, diseases had been cured, men had walked on the moon, and Canis and Hamstead had missed it all.

"Wait? Why are we here? I thought we were going to Faerie to save Puck," Daphne said.

"We are, *liebling*. The fairy kingdom is in New York City," Granny Relda replied.

Sabrina felt her face grow hot. The pavement seemed to shift and she fell forward. For a moment there was nothing but blackness and then she was on the ground looking up at her family.

"*Liebling*, are you OK?!" her grandmother cried. Mr. Canis

lifted Sabrina back onto her feet but the girl still felt dizzy and slightly nauseated. "You must have fainted."

"You didn't tell us there were Everafters in the city!" Sabrina said as she struggled to stand on her own.

Granny frowned. "Sabrina, Wilhelm's barrier didn't go up until twenty years after the Everafters arrived in this country. Some of them moved to other—"

"How many?" Sabrina demanded.

"How many what, child?" Granny Relda said.

"How many Everafters live here?"

"I don't know, Sabrina," the old woman replied, turning to Mr. Hamstead.

"Probably ten fairies and maybe five dozen others," the portly man said, after a long pause. "When Wilhelm was alive we kept in better contact with them but . . ."

Tears gushed out of Sabrina's eyes and froze on her cheeks. She prided herself on being strong, not a weepy girlie-girl, but she couldn't help herself. This was a shock. Ever since Granny Relda had taken them in, she had imagined that one day Daphne and she would return to the city with their parents and resume their old lives. They would look back on their time with the Everafters as a bad dream. Now she knew there was no escape from them.

"Sabrina, what's the matter?" Daphne asked.

Sabrina said nothing. Instead, she turned away from her family and stared out at the city skyline. The initial joy at seeing her home had disappeared. Now it seemed alien to her.

"It must be all the traveling," Granny said, rubbing Sabrina's back affectionately. "You girls are hungry and exhausted. We need to get you something to eat. Maybe some hot soup would help."

There was an uncomfortable silence among the group until Mr. Canis spoke. "First we must find Puck's people. Where is this Faerie?"

Granny sighed. "Unfortunately, the family journals are a bit thin on the Everafters that settled here. I do know Faerie is hidden somewhere in the city." She fished in her handbag and pulled out an envelope with some writing on it. "And a contact I have sent me this years ago."

Daphne took the envelope and read aloud, stumbling over some of the words.

Mrs. Grimm,

I'm sorry for your loss. Basil was like a father to me. It breaks my heart that I can't be there for Henry or you, worse that I am partially to blame for the tragedy. I hope you know that Jacob and I never believed that my escape from Ferryport Landing would bring anyone harm. I hope you can find it in your heart to forgive me.

I've found Faerie, which is hidden in the Big Apple. I've been invited to stay until I am settled. Oberon is very busy with his kingdom, and Titania, well, I'm sure you've heard the stories about her. Once I've found work and made a little money I'll be off to explore this big world. Until then, if you are ever in New York City, drop by the park and tell Hans Christian Andersen a knock-knock joke.

Love,

G

"Who's G?" Daphne asked.

"An old friend of your father's," Granny said. Sabrina and Daphne shared a knowing look. Their father had been in love with an Everafter before he met their mother, though everyone was tight-lipped about who the Everafter was.

"Can't we call this G person and get another clue?" Hamstead asked.

"Perhaps one that makes sense," Canis said.

"Is there anything else in the envelope?" Daphne asked.

Granny Relda looked inside. It was empty.

"We don't have time for this," Mr. Canis grumbled.

"It's all we have to go on," the old woman replied.

"Well, let's go find Hans Christian Andersen," Daphne said.

Granny shook her head. "Daphne, Andersen wasn't an Everafter. He just wrote about them. He died a long time ago."

"You know that, silly," Sabrina said. "We read it on his statue in Central Park."

"There's a statue of Hans Christian Andersen in Central Park?" Granny cried. "Sabrina, you're a genius. Can you take us there?"

Sabrina nodded reluctantly.

Once they were on their way again, Granny turned in her seat and handed the book she had been reading to Sabrina.

"You and Daphne should probably go through this," she said. "It's going to tell you everything you need to know about Faerie."

Sabrina glanced down at the book. It was a play by William Shakespeare, entitled *A Midsummer Night's Dream.*

Daphne snatched it and flipped through the pages. "What language is this?" she asked.

"It's English," Mr. Hamstead said. "Old English."

Minutes later they were over the bridge and cruising through the city's grid of streets and avenues. Book temporarily forgotten, Daphne gawked at the passing sites, pointing out her father's favorite diner and the playground their mother had taken them to on Sunday afternoons. Sabrina wanted to look out the window, too, but her old home was spoiled for her. There were few people who would describe New York City as normal, but now that Sabrina knew Everafters were crawling all over it, it seemed tainted, ugly.

Traffic was especially bad that afternoon. Christmas was only days away and everywhere shoppers were rushing into the streets carrying huge bags, slowing the family's progress dramatically. But they eventually made their way south through the city, and after much searching, Mr. Canis found a parking spot a few blocks from the park. As the family got out of the car, it rocked back and forth, angrily protesting with a series of backfires and exhaust clouds that caused some of the neighborhood residents to peer out their windows, apparently fearful there was a gun battle going on in the street. The family bundled Puck up in as many blankets as possible and trudged down a snowy sidewalk.

They made their way to the edge of the park and followed the stone wall until they found an entrance. Sabrina led them down a path that twisted and turned until they came to a man-made pond lined with benches. In the summertime, the pond was used by miniature-boat enthusiasts, who guided their tiny ships across its mirrorlike surface. Sabrina remembered her mother had loved this part of the park. Veronica had brought the girls there on many weekends and they spent hours watching the people walk by.

"Are you sure this is the place?" Mr. Hamstead asked.

Sabrina nodded and pointed across the pond. There sat a

bronze statue of Andersen himself. Dressed in a suit, tie, and top hat, he was looking down at his most famous story—the ugly duckling.

"I think your contact is playing a game with us, Relda," Mr. Canis snarled as they approached the statue. He eyed a suspicious-looking man sitting on a nearby bench, sipping from a bottle in a brown paper sack.

Granny Relda reached into her handbag for her folded directions and reread them aloud. "It says we're supposed to tell a knock-knock joke to Andersen."

Canis grumbled. "What is a knock-knock joke?"

"You don't know what a knock-knock joke is?" Daphne cried.

"He doesn't do jokes," Hamstead said.

"Well, it goes like this. Knock knock."

Mr. Canis said nothing.

"You're supposed to say 'Who's there?'"

"Why?"

"You just do," the little girl said.

Mr. Canis took a deep, impatient breath. "Who's there?"

"Cows go."

Again, Canis was confused.

"You're supposed to say, 'Cows go who?'" Granny explained.

"Fine!" Canis snapped. "Cows go who?"

"No they don't," Daphne said. "Cows go moo."

Hamstead snorted with laughter and Granny giggled, but Canis flashed them both an angry look and they stopped.

"Well, let's give it a try," Granny said as she stepped in front of the statue. "Knock knock."

Unfortunately, nothing happened.

"Maybe we shout it?" Hamstead offered, and then started shouting the words as loud as he could. The rest joined him, causing the man on the nearby bench to mumble "freaks," get up, and stagger away.

"Well, this is real fun," Sabrina grumbled. "Anybody else got an idea before they send the crazy wagon to pick us up?"

"Where's Daphne?" Granny asked.

Sabrina glanced around but her sister was gone. "Daphne!" she shouted, feeling a nervous pain in her belly. She hadn't been paying attention when she should have been! Daphne was her responsibility.

"I do not smell the child," Mr. Canis said.

"She was standing right here!" Sabrina cried, struggling with her panic.

Suddenly, Granny smiled and set her hand on the statue. "I've got an idea. Knock knock," she said, and in a blink, she vanished.

"I think we've found the front door," Mr. Hamstead said,

placing his hand on the statue as well. Canis joined him, shifting Puck in his arms to free a hand. Together the men said the magic words and they disappeared, too, leaving Sabrina alone on the snowy street. She looked into the great writer's face, took a deep breath, and secretly prayed that the family had indeed found a way into Faerie.

Knowing my luck I'll end up in the belly of a monster that enjoys goofy kid's jokes, she thought.

She reluctantly took a deep breath, and whispered, "Knock knock."

And then the statue's head turned to her, gave a big smile, and boomed, "*Who's there?*"

2

he world went fuzzy, as if Sabrina were looking at wavy lines on an old television. Just as quickly, her vision cleared and she found herself outside an old fashioned–looking restaurant. A neon sign above the door read THE GOLDEN EGG, and music and laughter could be heard from inside. Her family was nowhere in sight. Sabrina guessed they had gone inside to get out of the blistery cold. Before she could do the same, two chubby men appeared in the doorway. Each had big pink wings like Puck's, though the men were much older. One wore a burgundy tracksuit, the other a pin-striped two-piece. They shoved a short, naked man outside and he tumbled into the snow.

"How many times have we told you, Emperor? No shoes. No shirt. No service," the fairy in the tracksuit growled. "That means pants, too!"

"Yeah, this is a respectable establishment," the fairy in the pin-striped suit added. He had a face like a bulldog with hanging jowls and big bushy eyebrows.

"I *am* fully dressed!" the Emperor cried. His voice was slurred and he smelled like liquor. "You are just too stupid to see my clothes."

"The boss has banned you until you learn to obey the dress code!" bulldog-face grunted. He and his partner turned and went back into the bar, leaving the naked man lying in the snow, where he stayed for a few moments until finally crawling to his feet and stomping away. Sabrina could still hear him cursing as he disappeared from sight.

"That just scarred me for life," Sabrina said. Then she pushed the tavern door open and went inside.

The Golden Egg was a large, wood-paneled supper club, with tables, a long oak bar, and a fireplace. It had tin ceilings and smelled like steak and potatoes. At the tables sat roughly two dozen people of all shapes and sizes: an ogre played cards with a centaur, a princess quietly talked with six dwarfs, and a couple of men who seemed to be part human and part crow were arguing about politics. More folks were hunkered over tall frothy mugs at the bar, served by a woman with skin the color of coffee. At the back of the room was an enormous man with yellow eyes, playing a grand piano.

Sabrina scanned the room and quickly spotted her friends and family standing near the bar. She hurried through the crowd, almost tripping over a hedgehog riding a chicken. Perhaps it was the heat from the fireplace, but the Golden Egg was making Sabrina slightly ill. She felt as if she had walked into the pages of a bedtime story.

"Uh, where are we?" she asked when she joined the others.

"You're in the Golden Egg, honey," the bartender said as she washed some glasses. She was a pear-shaped woman with an apron wrapped around her waist and big, fluttery eyelashes. Her warm smile helped Sabrina's stomach relax a little. "We don't serve minors but I suspect I could find a glass of soda pop or two."

"Do you own this place?" Hamstead said over the bar chatter.

"Nope, I just run the place for the boss. People call me Momma. Haven't seen you in here before. You new in town?"

"We're looking for the fairy kingdom," Granny Relda said.

Momma laughed. "You've found it, lady. What's left of it, anyway."

"That can't be," Granny Relda said.

Sabrina scanned the room again. The crowd was sparse, and mostly drunk. It certainly didn't look like a fairy kingdom.

"Hey!" a voice said from below. Sabrina glanced down at her feet and nearly screamed in fright. Looking back at her was a

walking, talking gingerbread man no more than three inches high. "Watch where you're stepping, kid!"

Sabrina stared at the little baked good in horror. In the past three months she had talked to a lot of things that weren't supposed to be able to talk back. She was still not used to it and suspected she never would be. Her bellyache returned with a vengeance.

"What are you looking at?" the gingerbread man said to her. "Didn't anyone tell you it's rude to stare?"

For once, Sabrina fumbled for words.

"She's sorry," Daphne offered. "It's not every day you get to talk to a cookie, you know."

The gingerbread man's brown body suddenly turned red and his icing face crinkled in anger. "Hey! Cookies are round, buster. Do I look like I'm round?"

"Sorry," Daphne said. "I didn't mean—"

"That kind of ignorance is why gingerbread people are treated so badly all over the world," he said bitterly. "Just 'cause we all came out of the oven doesn't mean we're made from the same dough!"

Daphne ducked behind Sabrina.

"Relax! She didn't mean to offend you," Sabrina said, finally pulling herself together. As she turned to calm her sister, she felt something hard bounce off her head. She whipped around and found the gingerbread man pulling a gumdrop off his chest. There was one already missing—one she was sure was now lodged in her hair.

"Take that, you bakist!" the little man said.

"Did you just throw something at me?" Sabrina cried, quickly regaining her wits.

"Yeah! What are you going to do about it, meat person?" the little baked man taunted.

"Throw another gumdrop at me and you'll see what I'll do, dough boy," Sabrina hissed. Granny was trying to pull her away when the second gumdrop bounced off of Sabrina's nose.

"That's it!" she cried as she turned to the bartender. "Give me the biggest glass of milk you've got!"

The gingerbread man kicked Sabrina in the ankle. Despite his size, it hurt, and Sabrina reached down to grab him. The little man darted away and ran through the bar.

"Catch me if you can, stupid meat person!" he cried.

"Girls, leave him alone," Granny said.

"He started it," Sabrina said, picking the gummy candy out of her hair.

"Sorry, kid," Momma said from behind the bar. "He looks sweet but he's really hard to swallow."

The patrons at the bar let out a groan but Momma giggled at her joke like a little girl. "I got a million of them," she said.

"We have a sick fairy with us," Mr. Canis said impatiently. "He needs medical attention, now. Can you help?"

Momma pointed to the back of the bar. "Take him that way. The guards will let you in to see the boss."

"Who's the boss?" Hamstead said.

Sabrina glanced to the back of the room where the two guards Momma had referred to were standing. They were enormous.

"You folks really are from out of town," Momma said.

Granny Relda led the family over to the guards, who stood before two double doors. The men were so big they were nearly popping out of their suits. They wore dark sunglasses even though the bar was dimly lit.

"Yeah?" one of them growled.

"We need to see the boss," Granny Relda said.

"Sorry, lady," the other man said. "No one sees the boss."

"But—" Granny started to explain.

"Lady, dems da rules. Now push off."

"Listen," Mr. Hamstead said. "We were told to come here."

The guards looked at each other and then clenched their fists. "And I'm tellin' ya to leave," the first one said as he cracked his knuckles.

"We have a fairy here that needs medical attention," Canis growled.

The guard pulled the blanket away from Puck's head and then frowned.

"Absolutely not," he grunted.

"What?" Sabrina cried. "Why?"

"Puck is *liosta dubh*," the second snarled.

"What does that mean?" Daphne asked.

Sabrina shrugged. She usually knew the words Daphne asked about. She'd never heard *liosta dubh* before.

"It means he is unwelcome," the first guard snapped.

"If he doesn't get help he'll die," Mr. Canis barked.

"None of my concern. Now move along, geezer," the second guard said, giving Canis a rough shove.

"Pig, take the boy," the old man said calmly. Hamstead hurried to his side and took Puck in his arms just as the change came over Canis for the second time that day.

Granny Relda stepped over and rested her calming hand on his shoulder. "Old friend, I'm sure there is another way to—"

Before the old woman could finish, Mr. Canis's body had filled out his suit with rock-hard muscle. He towered over the guards now, yet they didn't seem at all anxious.

"Listen, grandpa," the second guard said with a yawn. "Your

little changing act don't impress me none. Move along before things get ugly."

Canis backhanded the man, sending him soaring across the tavern and smashing against a mirror that hung behind the bar. Bottles and glasses crashed down on the guard's head. Suddenly, the music stopped and all eyes turned to Sabrina and her family and friends.

"Oh, it's already gotten ugly," Canis snarled.

Much to Sabrina's surprise, the remaining guard went through a disturbing transformation of his own. His body doubled in size and his skin turned a muddy green. He grew pointy ears like a bat and his lower jaw jutted out past his nose. Two gnarled tusks like those on a saber-toothed tiger rose out of his mouth, and his eyes became as red as blood.

"Goblins!" Hamstead cried.

The guard held a knotty club, which he swung into Mr. Canis's chest as if he were trying to hit a home run. The blow was like a tiny annoyance to the old man, and he snatched the weapon away, crushing it into splinters in his furry hand. Then he seized the guard around the neck and lifted him off the ground.

"The boss will kill you," the first guard cried from behind the bar as he sprang to his feet. He was already changing into a beast as gruesome as his partner.

"I'd like to see him try," Canis said with a wicked laugh. "Do you think he can stand up to the Big Bad Wolf?"

A chill raced up Sabrina's back. Mr. Canis was certainly losing control of his alter ego if he was now referring to himself as the Big Bad Wolf.

"Control yourself, Everafter," bellowed a voice. Four fairies appeared from nowhere and surrounded the family. They were much more like Puck in appearance than the two fairies Sabrina had seen at the tavern door. Each had porcelain skin and blond hair. They all wore jeans, black boots, leather jackets, and ball caps, and would have looked like normal kids if it weren't for their pink wings and the crossbows they leveled at Mr. Canis's head. Each weapon was loaded with a jagged, steel-tipped arrow.

The leader of the group stepped forward. He had eyes like bright blue diamonds and a head of shaggy hair. His wings fluttered rapidly, as if responding to the tension in the room. He looked no older than Sabrina but had the confidence of a full-grown man.

"They are trying to get an undesirable in to see the boss," the second goblin croaked as he struggled to free himself from Canis's iron grasp.

"Release the guard," the fairy said to Mr. Canis.

Canis put the goblin down and then did something that made Sabrina shudder—he sniffed the creature and licked his lips.

"I smell your fear, darkling," he said to the guard. "It's delicious."

Granny set a hand on Mr. Canis's shoulder. "Old friend," she said softly, and this time it calmed the old man. He shrank to his familiar form but for a moment he glanced around as if he wasn't sure where he was. He looked down at his left hand with a confused expression. It had not changed back with the rest of his body. It was still covered in thick brown fur.

The fairy leader turned to Mr. Hamstead, who held Puck bundled in his arms. "Let's see this fairy."

Hamstead pulled back the blanket to reveal Puck's fevered face. The leader blanched, then gingerly took the weak boy into his own arms, cradling him gently.

"He's wounded, badly," Granny Relda said. "We hoped your people might be able to help."

"Follow me," the boy fairy said as his wings vanished.

"But Mustardseed," one of the guards cried. "Your father—"

Mustardseed turned a hard stare on the goblin. "My father will not hear of this, will he?"

The goblin's eyes were now alight with fear. "Of course not," he stammered.

The boy fairy nodded, turned, and strode through the double doors. The group hurried to follow. He led them down a long, narrow hallway lined with doors. At the far end was a pair marked EMPLOYEES ONLY. The fairy shouldered them aside and gestured for the family to follow.

They found themselves in a large room with hardwood floors. A roaring fireplace crackled on one side and a large oak desk sat on the other. A few high-backed chairs were scattered about. In one of them sat a woman wearing a leopard-print dress, big, golden hoop earrings, and matching shoes. Sabrina guessed she was in her early forties, and despite her gaudy outfit she seemed very dignified. She had long, brown hair, professionally styled, and the same shocking blue eyes as Mustardseed. A pretty young girl around Sabrina's age stood behind her, gently combing the woman's hair. The girl's eyebrows were arched upward in what appeared to be a permanent look of doubt and suspicion, and she was wearing an odd little pastel dress that seemed to be made out of silks and spiderwebs.

"Mustardseed, if you are looking for your father, he is not here," the woman said.

"Thank the heavens for miracles," the boy said as he set Puck on the nearest sofa. "Puck has returned."

The woman and the young girl cried out in unison, rose to their feet, and rushed to Puck's side. They knelt down and brushed his matted hair off his sweaty face.

"Son!" the woman cried.

Sabrina was stunned. She'd assumed that Puck had a mother—nearly everyone did—but she had pictured her as old and broken, physically and mentally exhausted by Puck's pranks and immaturity. This woman was young and healthy and seemed to be perfectly sane.

"Moth, find Cobweb—quickly!" the woman said to the girl. "Tell him to bring his medicines."

"But—"

"Go!" Puck's mother shouted. Moth cringed and raced from the room as the woman turned her attention back to Mustardseed. "Where did you find your brother?"

"You're his brother?" Sabrina said. "But you're so . . . clean." Puck was usually covered in food and whatever he had found in the forest to roll around in. *Puck has to be adopted,* Sabrina thought to herself.

"They brought him," Mustardseed said to his mother, gesturing to the Grimms.

"What did you do to my boy?" Puck's mother studied the group for the first time, her face full of suspicion.

"He was fighting a Jabberwocky and it ripped off his wings," Sabrina explained, feeling a lump of guilt lodge in her throat. He'd been trying to protect her.

The woman eyed her coldly. "And where would my son encounter a Jabberwocky?"

"Ferryport Landing," Daphne replied. "He lives there with us."

The woman scowled. "So, that's where he went."

"Ma'am, my name is Relda Grimm. I've been looking after Puck for some time, now. These are my—"

"*Grimm?* More troublemakers?" the woman bellowed, cutting Granny Relda off.

Sabrina sighed. Everywhere the family went they got an angry reception from Everafters. Was this just old hatred of Wilhelm . . . or had her father, Henry, been meddling in Everafter business? Sabrina's heart sank. Had her father been secretly doing the detective work he'd left Ferryport Landing to avoid?

"You must know our father, Henry," Sabrina said, testing her theory.

"Your father? No! I'm talking about Veronica Grimm," Puck's mother said.

"Veronica?" the Grimms cried in unison.

"You know our mom?" Daphne said.

The woman fell back as if she'd been slapped. "Veronica Grimm had children?"

At that moment, the little fairy girl known as Moth returned to the room. "Your Majesty, Cobweb is on his way."

"Very good. Mustardseed, escort these people to the street," his mother snapped. "Their presence is no longer required."

"Whoa, whoa, whoa!" Mr. Hamstead said. "Let's all calm down. Now we all want what is best for Puck, so—"

"You can leave on your feet or in a box," the woman threatened.

Mr. Canis stepped forward, eyes flashing. He started to open his mouth but was quickly interrupted by an angry voice.

"If anyone is leaving in a box it will be you!"

Sabrina spun around and found three large men standing behind her. Their leader was a tall, bearish fairy roughly the same age as Puck's mother. He had a big, thick face and thinning hair. He was wearing a black pin-striped suit, expensive shoes, and a gold watch. His wings were fluttering furiously. The other two men were the ones Sabrina had seen when she had first entered the Golden Egg, the track-suited bouncer and his bulldog-faced partner. They were carrying violin cases.

Their leader charged at Puck's mother, grabbing her roughly by the wrists and shaking her violently. "You've pushed me too far, Titania."

"Get your hands off me, Oberon!" the woman roared, pulling her hands away.

"Get this traitor out of here!" Oberon cried, pointing at Puck. His two huge cohorts moved toward the sick boy.

"He's hurt," Mustardseed said as he stepped in their path to protect his brother.

Oberon turned his anger on his son. "Would you like to join your brother in banishment? Do you want to be *liosta dubh,* as well?"

Mustardseed shook his head. Still, he stood his ground.

"Puck is your son and he's hurt, Oberon," Titania pleaded.

"He's no son of mine," the king snarled, standing over Puck's weak body with clenched fists. "He betrayed me. He turned his back on thousands of years of tradition. In the old lands, the King of Faerie would have had his head on a pike for such disobedience."

"What's a pike?" Daphne whispered to her sister.

"A long pointy stick," Sabrina replied quietly.

Daphne curled her lip.

"Just like your traditions, the old lands are dead and gone," Titania said.

"Bah!" Oberon cried. "Not for long!"

Just then, a tall, thin man with long, black hair and a dark face entered the room. His eyes were sunken and purple. He carried a black case in one frail hand.

"You called for me," he said.

"Cobweb, I'm afraid you've wasted a trip. We won't be needing any medicine today," Oberon said, dismissing the fairy with a flick of his hand.

Sabrina was stunned. Would he really let Puck die?

"No! Wait!" Titania cried. She pulled her husband aside and her voice suddenly softened. "Let Cobweb heal Puck and I will give you a present."

"What could you give me that I would ever want, Titania?"

"Power, Oberon," Titania said. "I can give you power over the entire community."

"I already control them," the fairy leader said with a laugh. His goons giggled with him.

"Perhaps, but you don't command their respect. I can give you something you've always wanted—their support," Titania argued. "I can give you something that will help you rebuild your precious Faerie kingdom."

"And what would that be?" Oberon said.

Titania gestured to Sabrina and Daphne. "The children of Veronica Grimm."

Oberon looked stunned for a moment, then laughed. "Another one of your lies."

Titania grabbed Sabrina roughly by the wrist. "Tell him who your mother was, human."

"Veronica Grimm," Sabrina said, yanking her hand away. "But I think you've got the wrong Veronica Grimm. She wasn't involved in any Everafter nonsense."

Oberon's eyes flashed so brightly Sabrina had to look away. Then he turned to Cobweb. "Heal the boy!" Oberon turned back to his wife. "But when he is well he can go back to whatever rock he has been living under for the last ten years."

Mustardseed and Moth looked saddened by Oberon's declaration, but Titania nodded and thanked him.

Oberon spoke to the fairy in the tracksuit. "Bobby Screwball, I need the Wizard."

Bobby Screwball nodded, reached into his violin case, and took out a long, thin stick with a big silver star on the end. He waved it in circles above his head and with a flick of his wrist a man suddenly appeared from nowhere. He was short and paunchy with thinning hair and a big, bulbous nose. He wore gray trousers, a white shirt, and an emerald-green apron covered in oil and dirt. He seemed completely bewildered, his eyes darting around the room in panic. Then he frowned.

"Aw geez, Your Majesty," the man cried in a thick Southern accent. "I was in a staff meeting. An entire group of trainee elves and Santa Clauses just saw me disappear into thin air. They're probably all freaked out. You may think that forgetful dust grows on trees, but you're wrong. It's very expensive and harder and harder to get!"

"Wizard, I need your particular talents," Oberon said. "Tonight we're having a celebration. I want to see every Everafter in town. Tell them I have . . . a special surprise for them."

"You're kidding me, right? A party? Tonight?" the Wizard cried. "Impossible. I can't just walk over and have the signal turned on. These things have to be planned."

The fairy with the bulldog face stepped over to the Wizard, grabbed him by the shirt collar, and pulled him close. "You're the Wizard. Nothing is impossible."

"Call off your goon!" the little man cried.

"Let him go, Tony Fats," Oberon said. The fairy frowned but released the squirming man.

"Fine! But don't expect a miracle," the Wizard grumbled.

"That's what I like to hear," the king said. He turned to his men and gestured at Sabrina and her family. "Keep them somewhere safe. We don't want the community's Christmas present damaged before they get it."

"Will do, boss," Bobby Screwball said as Oberon marched out of the room.

"I will need a little privacy with Puck," Cobweb said as he

opened his case. He removed several vials containing powders, a few empty glass jars, a mortar and pestle. Then he began mixing things in the mortar.

"Everyone out," Titania said as she exited the room. Moth and Mustardseed followed close behind, leaving the Grimms and their friends to trail reluctantly after the odd, fidgety Wizard and Oberon's henchmen.

The Wizard took out a silver box that looked like a remote control. He pushed some of the buttons quickly, and when an odd wheeze came out of it he shook it angrily. Then, he pushed some more and shoved it into his pocket. When he looked up he acted as if he was noticing the group for the first time. "Who are you people?"

• • •

Bobby and Tony Fats led the family out into the hallway. Sabrina felt Daphne slip her hand into her own and squeeze tight.

"Don't worry," Sabrina whispered to the little girl, wishing she could take her own advice. She had no idea what Oberon's henchmen were capable of. Both Tony Fats and Bobby Screwball had hands as big as pumpkins. They also looked and talked as if they had seen too many mobster movies.

"The boss wants you to wait in here," Bobby Screwball said when he stopped at one of the many doors in the hallway. He opened it and shoved everyone roughly inside. The room was full of boxes and extra tables and chairs that matched the furnishings in the main room. The two men were preparing to leave when Sabrina spun around on them.

"Wait a minute!" she cried. "You can't lock us up."

"We can't?" Tony Fats said to his friend. "I thought we just did." They both laughed.

"No, you can't," Mr. Canis growled as he stalked toward them.

Tony and Bobby opened their violin cases and took out their magic wands. They waved them threateningly and Mr. Canis took a step back.

"You're not very nice," Daphne said. "What kind of Everafters are you?"

"We're fairy god*fathers*," Tony Fats said.

"I've never heard of fairy godfathers."

"And that's just how we like it," Bobby Screwball replied. "Now, you sit in here and keep your mouths shut and no one will get hurt."

Bobby slammed the door. Sabrina rushed over and pressed her ear against it. She heard the lock turn and the men's muffled conversation. Daphne joined her and together the two girls strained to listen.

"Veronica was a real looker," Bobby said.

"She had great gams, too," Tony added.

"What does *gams* mean?" Daphne asked.

"They liked her legs," Sabrina replied. The men's voices faded away.

"This can't be good," Hamstead said.

"Relda, I could easily overpower them," Mr. Canis said.

"And we may need you to do just that, old friend," Granny said. "But they do have Puck and he is not well. I believe it would be wise to just wait and see what happens. I don't believe we are in any danger."

"Not in any danger?" Sabrina cried. "Oberon says he's giving us away to the Everafters. I think we should find Puck and break out of here now."

"I think we should stay. They seem to know Mom," Daphne said. "Wouldn't it be cool if she was a fairy-tale detective, too?"

"Don't be so gullible," Sabrina said.

"I'm not being gullible!" the little girl cried. "What does *gullible* mean?"

"It means you believe what anyone tells you. They couldn't have known Mom. Remember, this is Puck's family! The Trickster King! This is all some big joke of theirs."

"I'm not so sure," Granny said. "Your mother was a Grimm, after all."

"By marriage," Sabrina said a little louder than she meant to. "My mom was the only normal person in this family. She would never have gotten involved with Everafters!"

"Your mother knew about Everafters. She lived in Ferryport Landing with your dad when you were just born," Granny said.

"She's right, Sabrina," Hamstead said. "Your mother and Henry got into a number of adventures in the short time she lived with us."

"Adventures?" Mr. Canis grumbled. "More like near-death experiences."

"I think that's why she fit into the family so nicely," Granny Relda said with a smile. "Veronica seemed to have a healthy dose of the Grimm women's spunk."

"Stop it! Stop it! Stop it!" Sabrina cried. She felt she had to defend her mother. Nobody knew Veronica better than she did! The thought that she would have chosen to get involved in the family business when she didn't have to was ridiculous. Her mother was a normal, everyday, predictable person who enjoyed reading, museums, and her children. She was exactly what Sabrina wanted to be when she grew up.

"Well you don't have to be a jerkazoid about it," Daphne snapped.

"Jerkazoid?" Mr. Hamstead asked. Sabrina's little sister was always coming up with unusual words that made sense only to her.

"It's my new word. It means her jerkiness isn't normal—it's superpowered."

Sabrina ignored the little girl's insult and turned to her grandmother. "We should leave now," she pleaded.

Granny shook her head.

Sabrina wanted to argue but she could see it was pointless. When the old woman made up her mind there was no use trying to change it.

• • •

The family waited for over an hour in near silence. After some time, Bobby Screwball and Tony Fats brought them a supper of antipasti, salad, stuffed shells, and lemon chicken. It looked and smelled delicious, and Sabrina was starving, but she refused to take a bite, warning that it was probably poisoned. Mr. Canis sniffed it and assured her that there was nothing unusual about the food, but she still wouldn't eat.

Some time later, the door opened and the Wizard entered. He stepped into the room, wearing the same outfit as earlier, but he was quite a bit more frazzled. He looked as if he had spent the past hour pulling out what little hair he had left on his head.

"I'm very sorry about this, folks," the Wizard said.

Mr. Canis sprang on the little man, knocking him to the ground. Fangs dipped out of this mouth and hovered dangerously close to the Wizard's neck.

"We have questions," Canis growled. "And we're tired of waiting for answers."

"I don't know anything!" the Wizard cried. "I swear. Oberon sent me to retrieve you. The party is about to start."

Mr. Canis turned to Granny Relda who nodded. "Let him up."

Canis allowed the man to get to his feet. The Wizard brushed himself off, checked his neck for puncture wounds, then said, "Listen, I'm sorry this is happening but I'm just the messenger."

"And who exactly are you?" Hamstead asked.

"My name is Oscar Zoroaster Phadrig Isaac Norman Henkel Emmannuel Ambroise Diggs." He reached into his pocket, took out his silver remote, pushed a button, and waited as a business card spit out from a slot in the front. He handed it to Granny Relda.

"*The* Oscar Zoroaster Phadrig Isaac Norman Henkel Emmannuel Ambroise Diggs?" she said.

"The one and only," the man said.

"Are you an Everafter?" Daphne asked.

"Yes, ma'am. My friends have been known to call me Oz."

Daphne let out a squeal that sounded like a scream and a snort at the same time. She jumped around in a crazy jig. When she was finished she stood shaking and giggling with the palm of her hand firmly planted between her upper and lower teeth.

After a minute, she removed her hand, cried "You're my favorite," and launched herself at the stunned man. She wrapped her arms around him, and he tightened up as if the little girl were trying to kill him rather than give him a hug.

"Favorite what?" Oz asked.

"Favorite everything!"

"Well, it's always nice to meet a fan," he replied, struggling to free himself.

"Don't be too flattered," Sabrina mumbled. "She does the same thing when the pizza delivery guy shows up at the door."

Granny pulled the little girl away with considerable effort.

"I assume you all are from Ferryport Landing. We don't get to meet too many of our neighbors from the north," Oz said, quickly turning to Sabrina. "And I know you. You're Sabrina. I haven't seen you in years. Your mother used to bring you by the store all the time. I remember once we put you on Santa's lap to get a picture and you wet your pants. Santa was furious. Oh, your mother was so embarrassed, but I found it very funny."

Liar! Sabrina thought, blushing. She was tired of the game the

Everafters were playing with her. "My mother never worked in a store."

"Oh no, I work in a store, Macy's Department Store, actually. Your mother and I were great friends. She visited me there often." Oz turned to Daphne. "And you must be Daphne. I held you when you were no bigger than a snow pea. You both look so much like her. You are going to break a lot of hearts when you are older."

Daphne looked as if she was going to hug the Wizard again.

"Are we prisoners?" Granny Relda asked, gesturing toward the door.

Oz frowned. "The king would probably call you *guests*."

"Guests who aren't allowed to leave this room," Hamstead said. "Why?"

"I'm afraid I'm in the dark as well," Oz said. "Unfortunately, I'm the guy they call when they want something organized. They rarely tell me what it's for. But I promise that all of our questions will be answered soon. Right now, everyone is waiting for you."

He led the reluctant family down the hallway and back into the restaurant. Every seat was taken. It was one of the most unusual groups of people Sabrina had ever seen. There were pirates, dwarfs, goblins, talking animals, even an enormous man-size bug wearing glasses. A sultry blonde singer whose act brought catcalls and laughter from the audience had joined the yellow-eyed piano player. She wore a shimmering sequined dress and long, white gloves, and prowled around the room flirting with the male patrons. She flashed each a warm smile.

"She's beautiful," Hamstead said as he stared at the woman, dazzled.

"And off limits, if you know what's good for you," Oz said. "Her name is Bess. She's Tony Fats's girlfriend."

Just then, Oberon and Titania entered the room. Mustardseed, Cobweb, Moth, and the group of leather-jacketed fairies the family had met earlier followed in behind them. Their arrival brought forth a chorus of boos and jeers from the crowd, forcing the singer and the piano player to stop their lively performance.

"You've made us wait, Oberon!" an ogre shouted from his seat. "I've shared the same air with a Houyhnhnm for too long!"

A horse at the back of the room booed the ogre and spit at him.

"Why have you brought us here?" a chicken squawked from her seat. "I came all the way from Harlem."

"Friends, I have a present for you!" Oberon shouted as he moved through the crowd. "Christmastime comes to the Everafters."

The group exploded with anger. Many rose to their feet, shouting angry words about "dirty fairy tricks" and "not being fooled again." Oberon seemed unconcerned and just flashed the girls a grin. He rushed over to them, grabbed each roughly by the arm, and dragged them onto the stage at the back of the room.

"What's the big idea?" Sabrina said, trying to pull away from his powerful grip.

Oberon ignored her and turned to the crowd. "Silence!" he shouted. "Don't you want your present?"

Everyone sat back down.

"Yahoo no want present from fairy," yelled an incredibly hairy man.

"Is that so? You don't want the children of Veronica Grimm?" Oberon cried.

The crowd instantly hushed. They sat motionless, watchful and suspicious. Sabrina looked over at her sister and her heart began to race.

I knew it, she thought. *They hate us here just like they do back in Ferryport Landing. They're going to kill us.*

3

abrina took a deep breath and calmed herself. She had to be smart. She needed a plan to get herself and her sister out of danger. As she ran through the countless escapes they had made over the year and a half they were stuck in the foster care system, an answer popped into her head.

"Daphne, do you remember Mr. Drisko?" she said.

Daphne nodded.

"Let's give Oberon the Drisko treatment."

Mr. Drisko had been one of their more troubled foster parents. He was a certifiable nutcase who had made the girls share a bedroom with fifteen hyperactive ferrets. Sabrina had seen a documentary on television about ferrets. They were furry, adorable, and playful. The narrator had said they made excellent pets, but the narrator had never met Drisko's ferrets. Sure, they were cute but they were also evil. They bit Sabrina and Daphne every chance they got. They ate Sabrina's shoes and often relieved themselves on Daphne's pillow. Sabrina tolerated them for the sake of her sister, who needed a warm home, but it wasn't easy. Drisko said the ferrets were the loves of his life, and he doted on them like furry little babies. Unfortunately, Drisko's bad back and bunion-covered feet kept him from caring for the pets, so he had taken the girls in not out of charity but so that he would have a staff to feed and bathe his herd of messy, squeaky rodents. Sadly, it all fell apart when Mr. Drisko spanked the girls for refusing to give the ferrets pedicures. That's to say, he tried to spank them. He never laid a hand on them. He never got the chance.

"On three," Sabrina said.

Daphne nodded.

"One! Two! Three!"

Together the girls stomped down hard on the tops of Oberon's toes. The fairy king yelped in pain and bent over to rub his bruised feet. That's when the girls jumped on top of him and knocked him to the floor. They followed the tackle with a technique that had never failed the Grimm sisters—relentless kicking. By the time Granny Relda reached them, the girls had Oberon cowering on the stage in a ball.

"Are you OK, *lieblings?*" the old woman asked.

"We need to get out of here. This crowd is going to tear us apart!" Sabrina cried as she took her sister and grandmother by the hand. Tony Fats and Bobby Screwball were approaching, but if the family hurried, they could escape through the club's front door.

"Wait a minute! Do you hear that?" Daphne said, pausing at the edge of the stage. There was an odd noise coming from the crowd. It was laughter. The Everafters were laughing so hard that many were falling out of their chairs. Others applauded and rose to their feet. Soon they were all chanting the same word over and over again.

"Grimm! Grimm! Grimm!"

The Wizard rushed to Oberon's side and helped him to his feet. The fairy's face was red with rage. Oz whispered something in Oberon's ear and the anger drained away.

"They're just like their mother!" Oberon shouted as he hobbled toward the Grimm family. The crowd roared with laughter. "Turn the ovens on and prepare a feast. Tonight we celebrate the daughters of Veronica Grimm! Tonight her dream is reborn."

"What dream?" Sabrina asked, but no one answered. The Everafters rose to their feet and continued their chanting. They circled the girls, lifted them onto their shoulders, and marched around the supper club.

"What's he talking about?" Daphne asked Granny Relda, who hurried alongside.

Granny shrugged. "*Liebling,* I'm a bit confused myself."

"What a glorious day!" Oberon cried as the crowd set the two girls down in front of Oz and him, then rushed over to the bar where Momma had set down a round of celebratory drinks. "You two have no idea what you've done."

"I'm lost," Daphne said.

Oz responded. "I think what the king is trying to say is that your mother, Veronica Grimm, was highly respected in our little struggling community. When she was here she worked with us to keep Faerie alive. When she disappeared, well, so did the commitment to our way of life. We've lost our way, but you two could help put us all back on the right path."

"How?" Daphne said. "I'm only seven."

Before Oz could answer, Granny Relda spoke.

"Oberon, we didn't come here to get caught up in the politics of the city," she said. "As soon as Puck is better we need to get on our way. We have business at home that needs our attention."

"That's fine," Oberon said. "You can go back to wherever you came from right after dinner. We'll eat. We'll drink, and then all the girls have to do is back up everything I say. Afterward, I'll hand Puck over myself. You'll be on your way home before midnight."

"What do you mean 'back up everything' you say?" Hamstead said, suspiciously.

"Simple, just tell the Everafters that I'm in charge. Tell them Veronica always wanted them to recognize me as their king. Tell them that I'm supposed to lead the rebuilding of Faerie."

Sabrina glanced at Oz. His face suddenly darkened. He looked as if he wanted to argue but he held his tongue.

"Oberon, I'm afraid that's not possible," Granny Relda said.

Oberon scowled. "Why not!"

"Because we don't know if that is what Veronica wanted," the old woman said. "We didn't even know that she was involved with your community until this afternoon."

"And we have our doubts about that, too," Sabrina said. She still wasn't convinced that this wasn't a mean-spirited practical joke.

Oberon rose to his full height. His eyes flashed with anger and his mouth twisted into an ugly grimace. "You do what I tell you to do, you hear? This is too important and I don't have time to explain it to you."

"But—" Granny cried.

Oberon interrupted. "I still have Puck and I can cut off his cure at any time."

"Is that a threat?" Granny cried.

"It is what it is," Oberon snarled. "Tonight your girls are going to say what I tell 'em to say."

He spun around and marched through the chanting crowd. Oz gave them a pained smile and followed the fairy.

"What are we going to do?" Hamstead asked.

Granny shook her head. "I don't know, Ernest. I just don't know."

• • •

The celebration dragged on and on. The Everafters danced and drank. Momma poured glass after glass as quickly as she could. Sabrina noticed that like Mr. Hamstead, when Momma got excited she changed into her true form: an enormous black goose with a blue bonnet on her head. More than a few intoxicated guests ruffled her feathers, and she changed back and forth throughout the night.

The girls were nearly as busy. Everyone wanted to shake the hands of Veronica's girls. (Sabrina was sure someone was going to yank her arm off at any moment.) They all had stories, too. Each Everafter shared a tale about their mother and how she had inspired or helped them; each story broke Sabrina's heart. As much as she wished it weren't true, it grew more and more obvious that Veronica had been a part of the Everafter community of

New York City. Every story chipped away at the symbol her mother had become to Sabrina, of average, everyday, normal life, free of chaos and lunacy. Each story felt like a thief that crept in to steal her hopes and dreams.

And what to make of Oberon's demands? Sabrina didn't know much about the Everafters, but she knew she didn't like Oberon. Judging from the crowd's response to him earlier that evening, it seemed as if the Everafters shared her sentiment. Oberon was a jerkazoid, as Daphne would have said. But could he be telling the truth? Could her mother have actually supported him in his power grab? She couldn't be sure because she had no idea who her mother was anymore. And even if Oberon was lying, what could Sabrina and Daphne do? He had Puck.

While the girls were listening to praise from a woman who appeared to be wearing a dress made out of donkey skins, Oz came over and ushered the girls to a quiet corner. He looked even more nervous and fidgety than before. He pulled out his silver remote and pushed some buttons. The device let out a few loud squeals. Then Oz turned back to the girls, took Sabrina and Daphne by the hands, and looked deeply into their eyes.

"Girls, your mother was one of the best friends I ever had, and it pains me to think that tonight Oberon will finally snuff out her legacy," Oz said. "The king is a fraud. He's lying to you.

The last thing in the world Veronica Grimm would have wanted was for him to lead this community."

"What do you want us to do about it?" Sabrina asked. "You heard his threat. He'll stop Cobweb from helping Puck."

Oz peered around the room, again.

"Girls, just tell the truth. Tell the crowd you never knew your mother's plans but you're sure she would never have wanted Oberon to rule. It will destroy any support he has from the community. After that, I'll create a diversion and in the chaos I'll take you to Puck. Then you can head back to Ferryport Landing. Cobweb has told me the boy is out of the woods and can be moved."

"This sounds dangerous," Sabrina said.

"Good," Daphne said, rubbing her hands together eagerly. The little girl was fearless.

Oz smiled. "Veronica would be proud of you." He said his good-byes and slunk back into the crowd.

• • •

Soon, Everafters were pulling tables and chairs together, making one long banquet table and covering it with food, candles, and malted beverages. Puck's brother, Mustardseed, appeared.

"Puck is safe," he said, confirming what Oz had already told them. He escorted the girls to seats at the head of the table.

They sat down just as bowls of pasta with red sauce and plates of steaming meat were placed in front of them.

"Is this all-you-can-eat?" Daphne cried. "I'm starving!"

Mustardseed smiled and nodded. Canis, Granny Relda, and Hamstead found seats next to theirs.

Bess, the beautiful blonde singer, took a seat next to Mr. Hamstead. On her other side was Tony Fats, who had already started eating. Bess glanced at Hamstead and smiled. He smiled back, but his already pink face flushed red and he turned away. The poor man was flustered.

"What's wrong with you?" Sabrina whispered into his ear. "Are you sick?"

"She smiled at me," Hamstead squeaked, nodding in the blonde beauty's direction. "What's she doing, now?"

"She's looking at you and smiling," Daphne replied. "She thinks you're foxy."

Hamstead's pig snout sprang onto his face and he quickly covered it with his hand. "Get a hold of yourself, Hamstead," he muttered to himself.

Titania swept into the dining room. Mustardseed helped her to her chair at the far end of the table and then took a seat next to her. Even from that distance, Sabrina could see the angry scowl on Titania's face. It was directed right at her and her family.

Oz rushed in from one of the back rooms and over to Sabrina. "Everything is all set," he whispered to her.

"What's the diversion?" Sabrina whispered to him, but before he could answer a chicken hopped into a nearby chair and flapped its wings furiously.

"Where's Oberon?" the chicken cackled as it slurped down some fat purple worms.

"Patience, Billina," Oz replied. "He's on his way."

Just as the Wizard leaned down to whisper to Sabrina again, there was a loud scream. The door leading from the back hallway burst open and Moth rushed into the room. Her face was twisted and red from crying and her beautiful hair was flying in all directions. She fell to her knees in despair and beat the floor with her fists. "It's Oberon! It's the king!"

Titania stood up so quickly she knocked over her heavy chair. "What is this nonsense?"

"I found him in his office. He's been poisoned. He's dead!"

"Impossible!" someone shouted.

Titania rushed around the table and raced into the back hallway with Mustardseed close behind. The dinner guests jumped to their feet, knocking chairs and plates over in their excitement.

"Is this the diversion you were talking about?" Sabrina shouted at Oz.

The Wizard looked dumbstruck. "No! I have no idea what is going on!"

Granny Relda grabbed the girls and quickly found her way to the back hall. Together, they pushed through the crowd of Everafters at the door to Oberon's office. The sight inside made the blood freeze in Sabrina's veins. The king was lying on the floor next to his desk, a shiny gold cup clutched in his hand. His face was contorted in agony, as if the last moments of his life had been excruciating torture.

Titania threw herself on top of her husband and wailed with despair. She screamed as if it were she who had been fatally wounded. Mustardseed tried to help his mother up but she fought him off ferociously, and he backed away to let her grieve.

"Who killed my husband?" Titania cried. Sabrina was too distracted to listen. For there on Oberon's chest, in bright red paint, was a handprint. It was the mark of the Scarlet Hand.

4

abrina had never seen anger in a person's face like she saw in Titania's. The queen's rage seemed to pour out through her eyes and spill onto the crowd like acid. Everafters fell backward just to avoid her gaze.

"One of you killed my husband!" Titania cried, rising to her feet with clenched fists. "Who is responsible? Who has blood on his hands? Will no one come forward? Then I'll avenge my beloved by killing you all." The queen's body underwent a terrifying metamorphosis. Her already pale complexion turned bone white. Tar-black veins curled in all directions just underneath her skin, weaving along her arms, legs, and head. Her hands grew to three times their normal size, and long, jagged nails, several feet in length, shot out of the fingertips. Her hair blazed with actual flames, and long, blue cables of electric energy crackled and popped in the air in front of her eyes. Her wings sprang out of her back and flapped so hard they seemed to shake the room. She rose above the crowd, opened her mouth, and sprayed the room with a fiery liquid. Anything it touched was quickly engulfed in flames and reduced to cinders.

Everafters shrieked and stampeded toward the door, knocking the smallest in the crowd to the ground. Mr. Canis snatched the girls up, tucking them under his arms like footballs, and ran.

"We have to get out of here," Granny Relda shouted as she was shoved aside by Tony Fats and Bobby Screwball, who ploughed through the crowd, desperate to escape Titania's wrath.

"Wait," Hamstead called to the old woman, turning and rushing back toward the queen.

"Ernest, are you crazy?" Granny Relda called after him, but he didn't stop.

From Mr. Canis's grasp, Sabrina looked back to see the portly man run to the side of the blonde singer he had sat next to at dinner. Bess had been knocked to the ground and was cowering before Titania's murderous gaze. Her boyfriend, Tony Fats, had left her to die.

"*No!*" Hamstead cried as he grabbed a heavy chair and used it to fend off Titania. The queen shrieked and ignited the chair with her fiery breath. If Hamstead was afraid, he didn't show it. He tossed the flaming chair at the queen and then turned to help Bess to her feet. Together they raced out of the room just behind Canis and the Grimms.

When the group reached the main room they paused, and Hamstead asked Bess, "Are you OK, ma'am?"

"*Ma'am* is a name for old ladies," she said as she tried to catch her breath. "You can call me Bess, cowboy."

Hamstead blushed.

"We need to keep moving," Mr. Canis said.

"We can't leave without Puck!" Daphne cried.

Mr. Canis snarled and set the girls down. "Hamstead, take Mrs. Grimm and the girls to safety. I'll join you once I find the boy."

"I'm coming with you," Sabrina said.

Canis shook his head.

"It's my fault Puck got hurt in the first place. He's my responsibility," Sabrina said, hoping that the old man could see she wasn't asking for his permission.

"Stay close," he said, shoving back through the crowd.

Sabrina followed at his heels, struggling against a tide of panicked Everafters. She craned her neck in hopes of spotting Cobweb, the fairy who was tending to Puck, but he was nowhere in sight. He and Puck had to be in one of the rooms that lined the back hall. Canis cleared a path through the main room to the hallway.

"Maybe Puck's in there," Sabrina shouted to Canis over the melee, pointing to the first closed door. She rushed over and turned the knob, but it was locked tight.

Canis turned the knob himself. It fell off in his powerful hand, and he pushed the door open. It was a broom closet filled with mops and bottles. Sabrina rushed across the hall to another door, also locked. Again Canis crushed the knob. They found Moth pacing a room in which sat what looked like a giant eggplant. It had deep purple skin with green veins running through it. Next to it was a small table covered in potions and powders. When she saw them, the fairy girl ran to the eggplant as if to protect it.

"How dare you invade my room!" she cried.

"Where's Puck? We have to get out of here," Sabrina said. Canis closed the door behind them. "Titania has gone crazy. She's trying to kill everyone."

"Titania won't hurt me."

Mr. Canis let out a loud growl. "Because I'll get to you first!" he barked. "Where is the boy?"

The fairy girl's eyes grew wide with fear and she gestured at the eggplant. "He's right there!"

"That's Puck?" Sabrina said, incredulously.

"He's in a cocoon stage as his wings heal," Moth explained.

Just then, something heavy slammed against the door, nearly knocking it off its hinges.

"She's coming," Mr. Canis said.

"How are we going to get out of here?" Sabrina cried.

Mr. Canis searched the room for other exits but found none. He turned to Sabrina and for a moment she thought she saw worry in his face. Then, his body grew in size. His face seemed more wolflike, as if he were somewhere between the old man she knew and the wolf she feared. He stepped over to the far wall and pounded it with his enormous hand. It crumbled and a small hole appeared. He smashed the wall again, this time making the hole big enough to step through.

"Girls, come with me," he growled, and though Sabrina was afraid of his appearance, she was more afraid of the monster trying to get into the room. She raced over to the cocoon and snatched it in her arms. It was surprisingly light and had a horrible smell like moldy pickles.

"Who are you, Everafter?" Moth shouted at Canis.

"He's the Big Bad Wolf," Sabrina explained.

"The murderer?" the fairy girl shrieked. "I'm not going anywhere with you!"

Just then, the door to the room blew off its hinges. Titania appeared in the doorway, her mighty wings vibrating the air. She roared like a lion and shot a stream of fire right at them.

"Suit yourself," Sabrina said, tightening her grip on the cocoon. She turned and ran through the opening in the wall with Mr. Canis following close behind. Moments later, Moth came flying frantically after them, her pink insectlike wings keeping her aloft.

They were back in the park where Daphne had first told the knock-knock joke that had revealed the Golden Egg. The restaurant had disappeared again. Sabrina had left her coat inside, and now she was freezing. She hurried alongside Canis, doing her best not to fall in the slippery snow, but it wasn't easy. She turned her ankle and almost lost her hold on Puck's cocoon. Moth landed in front of her and snatched the cocoon out of Sabrina's hands. "You have no right to touch His Majesty's healing vessel," she said indignantly.

"Fine! Keep the stinky thing!" Sabrina said as she scanned the area. Where could they hide?

Suddenly Titania appeared behind them, as if out of thin air. She soared overhead, preparing to strike.

Mr. Canis rushed over to one of the lamps that lined the park paths and pulled it out of its concrete mooring. There were several loud pops as the electrical wires inside were ripped apart.

Canis swung the lamp like a bat right at the queen and hit her hard. She was hurled into the pavement with enough impact to create a smoking crater. Canis stood over the hole, waiting for Titania to crawl out.

Granny, Daphne, Hamstead, and his new friend Bess appeared nearby and rushed to join Sabrina. Granny looked worried. "We should go," she said.

"Haven't I been saying that all day?" Sabrina cried.

No sooner were the words out of her mouth than Titania rose out of the crater and screamed like a banshee.

"Any suggestions?" Canis asked.

Sabrina turned to Moth. "What should we do? She's going to kill us all."

"She won't kill me," the fairy said. "I'm a princess."

Sabrina scowled. If they survived, she needed to remember to introduce Moth to her fist. Just then, Mustardseed and his fairies appeared in the sky and surrounded Titania. They threw long, thick ropes around the queen, binding her as she fought and screamed. Mustardseed's men dragged her toward the spot where the Golden Egg had been and disappeared once again into the invisible restaurant.

Mustardseed landed next to Granny. "You must leave here," he said. "I will take my brother."

"Forget it," Sabrina said. "Puck stays with us."

"I'm not arguing with you, child," Mustardseed said angrily.

"Then don't. I'm not letting him anywhere near your mother," Sabrina said.

"I'm confused," Granny said to Sabrina. "You're talking as if Puck is with us."

"He is," Sabrina said, pointing at the cocoon Moth was holding.

"This is Puck?" Daphne said, placing her hand on the cocoon's skin. A sticky trail of goo clung to her fingers when she pulled it off. "Oh yeah, this is Puck all right."

"Mustardseed, as Puck's fiancée I will look after the crown prince," Moth said.

"Fiancée?" everyone cried.

Mustardseed thought about this for a long moment, seeming to weigh his options, then nodded reluctantly. "You may take him," he said to Granny, "if you take Moth, too, and keep them both safe. But do not take Puck from the city."

"Sorry, buddy. We're out of here now!" Sabrina cried.

"Do not leave the city!" Mustardseed roared.

Granny Relda nodded. "We'll stay."

The fairy looked relieved. "I must go to my mother," he said, and he turned and flew back toward the restaurant, disappearing in a blink.

Granny took the opportunity to usher everyone out of the park. When they were several blocks away, she stopped to catch her breath.

"We should go back to the car and drive away from here as soon as possible," Sabrina said, shivering. "We have Puck. There's no reason to stay. If we stick around, someone is going to get hurt."

Mr. Canis removed his suit jacket and wrapped it around Sabrina to keep her warm. Daphne, who was also without a coat, squirmed inside, too, wrapping her arms around her sister.

"I agree with the girl," Canis said.

"We can't go! This is a mystery," Daphne said. "They might need our help solving it."

"Another good reason to leave!" Sabrina said.

"Daphne's right," Granny said. "We'll check into a hotel. We all saw the mark on Oberon's chest. The Scarlet Hand is behind his murder."

Before Sabrina could argue, Tony Fats buzzed the group and landed next to Bess.

"I'm glad you got out OK, Bess," he said.

"No thanks to you," she replied. Then she sighed, turned to Mr. Hamstead, leaned in close, and kissed him on the cheek.

"Thanks, cowboy," she said. "What do they call you?"

"My name's Ernest," Hamstead said, as he turned pink.

Tony Fats grumbled, snatched his girlfriend by the wrist, and dragged her back down the street as Hamstead looked on wistfully.

Granny raised her hand and a taxi pulled over. "We need to find a hotel with a parking lot for a car," she said to the driver. He shook his head and told them if they had a car to leave it where it was. "Parking is insane, lady," he explained.

Granny shrugged and helped Sabrina, Daphne, Moth, and Puck's cocoon into the back of the cab, then climbed into the front passenger seat. She rolled down the window and said to Mr. Canis and Hamstead. "Can you two find your own cab?"

"Relda, I believe I'll walk," Canis replied. He looked shaken and out of sorts. "The winter air will help my condition. I can follow your scent."

"I'll go with him," Hamstead said. "I'd like to see as much of the city as I can before we have to head back. I'll see you at breakfast?"

Granny nodded. "Take care." She rolled up her window and the cab pulled away.

"Is that the thing that is stinking up my cab?" the driver asked, looking at the purple orb in his rearview mirror.

"It's a school project," Sabrina lied. "Science fair stuff."

"What's the project? How quickly can you make a full grown man lose his lunch?"

"Hey, it's no rose garden back here, either," Sabrina said. "You ever clean this cab?"

The driver grumbled and turned his attention back to the road.

Soon, the cab pulled up outside the Fitzpatrick Manhattan Hotel and the women clamored out. The hotel was a tall, old-fashioned building with an emerald-green awning. The smell of tobacco drifted from inside. A doorman invited them into the warm lobby where several tourists sat in front of a crackling fireplace, looking out the window at the falling snow.

"My goodness," one of the tourists cried as she pinched her nose. "I think the sewers are backing up."

"Ugh, it smells like someone died," another complained.

Granny ignored the reaction to the cocoon and approached the front desk, requested three rooms, and asked that sets of keys be left for Mr. Hamstead and Mr. Canis. A bellhop looked at the family with an odd expression when he was told they had no luggage. He took them up to their room on the fourth floor. Inside they found two queen-sized beds, a bathroom with a marble tub, and a pamphlet on the sights and sounds of the Big Apple.

"This is unacceptable," Moth said before they had even

turned the lights on. "I am royalty and accustomed to refinements. We need to find a more suitable room for the prince and I! One that is private!"

Sabrina rolled her eyes and flipped on the light switch.

"Hello, Mrs. Grimm," a voice said from across the room. The women let out a shriek and nearly fell over themselves. There, sitting in a chair by the window was Mustardseed. Oz stood behind the fairy prince. "I hope that none of you was harmed this evening," Mustardseed said. "I'm sure you can understand that my mother's actions were due to stress and heartbreak."

"Well, she nearly flame-broiled us back there!" Sabrina cried.

"Yeah, she's a jerkazoid!" Daphne added.

Oz stepped forward. "But she was the only one of us who was thinking clearly at the time. Her only choice was to run everyone off. She had to allow the killer a chance to escape."

"Escape?" Granny cried. "Why on earth would she want to do that?"

"To protect the new king," Mustardseed said. "Otherwise, the killer might have hurt the heir to the Faerie throne."

"What's an *heir?*" Daphne asked.

"Someone who inherits something from a relative," Sabrina explained, then turned back to Mustardseed. "But I thought there wasn't a Faerie anymore."

"Faerie exists in our hearts and hopes," Mustardseed explained. "Some day we will find a way to rebuild it. Then we will need our king."

"So you're saying your mom was trying to barbeque us so she could protect you?" Daphne said.

"You are confused," Mustardseed said. "I am not the heir to the crown of Faerie. That honor falls to Puck."

"Puck is the new king?" Granny said, astonished.

Mustardseed nodded. "Protecting Puck was my mother's greatest concern. I knew you could be trusted to keep my brother safe. After all, you brought him here."

"Well, I hope Titania doesn't think we killed Oberon," Granny said.

Oz nodded. "We know that. Oberon was poisoned."

"With a concoction only a fairy could make," Mustardseed added. "It takes something very powerful to kill an Everafter. The ingredients for this particular poison came from the original fairy homeland and the recipe is one passed down within our kind. Only fairies and a few Everafters know it."

"And do you have any suspects?"

Mustardseed shook his head. "My father had many enemies."

"We suspect it was a fairy, or someone aided by one," Oz said.

"Unfortunately, whoever it was is now free on the streets of New York City. We know your reputation as detectives. We could use your family's help in finding the murderer."

Sabrina tried to wrap her head around this task. New York City had over eight million people living in it. It encompassed five different boroughs, linked by hundreds of miles of subway lines. Sure, Sabrina had grown up here, but there were so many streets and neighborhoods, no one could know them all. This wasn't Ferryport Landing, where they knew everyone. They didn't know these urban Everafters or even where they lived in the city. The job seemed impossible.

"This is not going to be easy," Granny said, obviously sharing similar thoughts.

"If you are half as resourceful as Veronica, I will have no worries at all," Mustardseed said.

"Folks, I'm afraid we've got one more favor to ask," Oz said. "Puck might be the killer's next target and after today's fiasco, we're pretty confident that you people can handle just about anything, including guarding him. He won't be safe at the Golden Egg."

"Of course, he's like one of my own grandchildren," Granny said.

Mustardseed rose from his seat. "Moth, you will stay with the Grimms. You will watch over your betrothed and assist the Grimms in any way they might need."

"As you wish, Your Majesty," the little fairy said with a deep bow.

"Oh, this is just getting better by the second," Sabrina said sarcastically.

Mustardseed turned to Granny Relda. "I want to be kept abreast of every development. I will be quite busy, so you can report your findings to Oz at the store in which he works." He bowed deeply, then turned to the window, opened it, and leaped out into the night. Above the howl of the wind, Sabrina could hear the sound of mighty wings flapping. Oz turned and closed the window tight.

"Any idea where we should start?" Daphne asked him.

The Wizard shook his head. "We don't exactly have an Everafter phone book."

"Then how did you get them all to meet at the Golden Egg tonight?" Sabrina said.

"I use the Empire State Building as a signal," Oz explained. "You may have seen them light it up for holidays. On Christmas they use red and Saint Patrick's Day it's green. When we need to see everyone we use bright purple."

"Perhaps we should try that," Granny said.

"I doubt anyone would show up after Titania's fit. I can tell you this much: I know the dwarfs live in the subway system and I believe Sinbad lives somewhere down by the docks," Oz said. "We Everafters keep to ourselves here in the city."

"That's it? That's all you know?" Sabrina cried.

"I'll ask around about the others and let you know if I find out anything else," the little man said. He apologized, said his good-byes, and moments later he left the room.

"We're in the middle of a mystery!" Daphne clapped, nearly bouncing in anticipation. "Where do we start?"

"Let's make a list of our clues so far," Granny Relda replied. "Sabrina, could you find us an ink pen? I bet there's one in the desk."

"No," Sabrina whispered. "I don't want anything to do with this. We should all just go home."

The room grew quiet. Daphne and Granny Relda stared at her as if she were some kind of algebra problem with no solution. Sabrina had rarely felt so alone. Couldn't Granny see that ever since she and Daphne had gotten involved in the detective business, they had been like two human wrecking balls, causing death and destruction over and over again? They had survived the Jabberwocky by the skin of their teeth and now they were jumping back into the fire. What if someone got hurt again?

What if their luck finally ran out? The sting of tears filled Sabrina's eyes and she quickly turned and ran into the bathroom, closing the door behind her. She sat on the side of the tub in the dark and tried to catch her breath.

After a few minutes, there was a knock on the door and it slowly opened.

"*Liebling?*" Granny Relda said as she flicked on the light and entered the room. She sat down next to Sabrina and put her hand on the girl's shoulder. Sabrina pulled away.

"I don't want to do this," she said to her grandmother.

"Sabrina, these people asked for our help. It won't hurt us to look around and ask some—"

"No . . . I'm not talking about this mystery. I don't want to be a Grimm."

Granny sat quietly for a long time and Sabrina prepared herself for a lecture about responsibility and doing the right thing.

"You don't have to, Sabrina," Granny finally said.

Sabrina was stunned.

"You were deposited into this life against your will. I thought that after some time you would get used to being a Grimm and see what a rewarding life it can be. But I realize now that I'm forcing you to do it and that isn't fair. You do have a choice and I should have explained it. Many in our family have walked away from their heritage. If you've ever read any of Douglas Grimm's journals, he often wrote about how miserable he was; even your Opa Basil had his doubts. Obviously, your own father made a choice to pursue a different life. You can do the same if that is what you want."

"Sure, and you'll be disappointed with me. You'll give me that look you give me when you're angry," Sabrina said.

"I'll miss sharing the time with you," Granny said. "And I truly believe you are becoming an excellent detective, but you can retire if you want. Perhaps it is best if you stay at home from now on and keep an eye on your parents."

Sabrina wondered if her grandmother was pulling a trick on her, but the old lady just smiled and kissed her on the forehead.

"I can still help find a way to wake up Mom and Dad?" Sabrina said.

"Of course," the old woman said.

Sabrina felt like the sun had come out and was shining just for her. The gnawing pain in her belly subsided for the first time in months.

"I can't wait to tell Daphne we don't have to do this anymore," Sabrina added.

Granny frowned. "Sabrina, you get to make your choice and you have to let her make one for herself."

"She's only seven years old," Sabrina argued.

"And you're only eleven, but I'm trusting your decision," the old woman said.

"But—"

"Now, unfortunately, we're in the middle of a case to which I have committed us all. So, let's make a compromise. When we get home you'll be done with being a fairy-tale detective, but right now, we have a mystery to solve. Can your sister and I count on you for one more case?"

Sabrina nodded. Still, she was happy; in fact, she was grinning from ear to ear. She hadn't expected her grandmother to understand her choice, let alone support it. She could walk away from the Grimm family legacy. No more Everafters, monsters, and lunatics. Now all she had to do was convince Daphne to make the same decision.

Granny Relda kissed Sabrina on the top of her head. "Let's go join the others."

The two women got up and left the bathroom. They found Mr. Hamstead had arrived. He explained that Mr. Canis wasn't feeling well and had gone to bed.

"Ernest," Granny Relda said. "I'm afraid we're going to be staying through tomorrow at least. Mustardseed has asked us to find his father's killer."

"Of course we'll help," Mr. Hamstead said.

Daphne clapped her hands. "What's the plan?"

"The plan, Daphne, is to get some rest. Tomorrow we're going to track down a killer."

"Where are we going to start?" Sabrina asked as she looked out the window at the massive city.

"At your old apartment," Granny replied.

• • •

The plan for the morning was to split up. Hamstead would search the lower part of the city and the Grimm family would handle the upper part. Mr. Canis was staying at the hotel for the day. When they had knocked on his door, he'd opened it just a crack and told Granny Relda that he needed time to meditate. She agreed that he should rest. Sabrina wondered if she'd noticed the new wolfish whiskers on the old man's chin.

When the group finished breakfast and met in the lobby, they were surprised to find they had a visitor. Bess was sitting in a chair by the fireplace. She had on a long winter coat and a silver backpack. She also had the coats Sabrina and Daphne had abandoned at the Golden Egg.

"Care for a little help?" Bess asked as she smiled at Hamstead.

"Of course," Hamstead stammered. "But won't this cause some waves with your boyfriend?"

Bess winked. "Ernest, I don't have a boyfriend anymore."

"We're happy to have the help," Granny said, shaking Bess's hand. "Why don't you team up with Ernest?"

"An excellent plan," the blonde woman said.

As the group stepped out of the hotel, they found that two feet of snow had fallen in the night, turning the city into a winter wonderland. Hamstead and Bess went in one direction while Granny, the girls, and Moth searched for a cab. After ten minutes without success, they caught a bus that took them uptown to the girls' old neighborhood on the Upper East Side. Unfortunately, where Moth went, Puck's smelly cocoon went, too. No one wanted to sit next to the slimy thing, which had begun to leak a funky gas not unlike rotten eggs, so the family spent the trip avoiding the angry looks of other passengers.

"Well, it seems as if your mother had a secret life," Granny Relda said as the bus headed up Madison Avenue. "Several of us have gotten into the family business through marriage. I'm a very good example, myself. So, if Veronica was working with Everafters like every other Grimm since Jacob and Wilhelm, she probably also wrote down what she was experiencing."

"You mean a journal? Do you think she kept one?" Daphne said. It was the family tradition to write one's adventures down so that future descendants might learn from them. Sabrina had a journal, too, though she rarely kept track of what she had encountered. Writing it down made it real. Daphne on the other hand was working on her second volume.

"I bet she did," Granny said. "And I suspect Veronica kept her activities secret from your father. When he left Ferryport Landing, he was dead set on building an Everafter-free life. If she had a journal she probably hid it. So it might still be in your old apartment."

"Is this place nearby?" Moth groaned. "The constant jostling of this vehicle is upsetting my delicate constitution."

"What did she say?" Daphne asked her sister.

"She's complaining," Sabrina explained. "Again."

After several stops, they finally reached the corner of Eighty-eighth Street and Madison Avenue and started walking east, toward York. This was a quiet little nook of the city filled with families, dogs, and older people. As Sabrina looked around, a wave of memories flooded over her. There was the little deli that sold the roast beef and gravy sandwiches her father snuck out to buy late at night. Down the street was Carl Schurz Park, where her family had spent many afternoons looking out on the East River or playing with the puppies in the little dog run. Across the street was the luxury apartment high-rise their mother often dreamed they'd live in one day. Sabrina spotted Ottomanelli's

Italian Eatery with its amazing meatball pizza, the dry cleaner where the Cuban lady always gave her lollipops, and the magazine store owned by the guy who let his three cats sleep on stacks of the *New York Times.* Sabrina could even smell the world's best brownies from Glaser's Bakery a block away. Little had changed, except that the old skateboard store was now a manicure shop.

They walked up Eighty-eighth Street, past a group of five-story brownstones, and quickly reached their old apartment building at number 448. It had recently been painted a gray-blue in place of the dirty yellow she remembered.

"We can't get in," Sabrina said, as they climbed the freshly salted steps. "The police took our keys when they sent us to the orphanage."

"Sabrina, those old keys wouldn't work anyway," her grandmother said. "There's a new family living here and I'm sure they've changed the locks."

Sabrina stifled a cry. She had never imagined that strangers might actually be living in their home.

"So someone else lives here?" Daphne whispered. Sabrina could hear her own dismay echoed in her sister's voice.

Granny nodded as she pushed on the buzzer that rang their old apartment.

"Hello, who is it?" a voice crackled from a speaker.

"Um, yes, so sorry to bother you, ma'am, but my name is Relda Grimm. I'm here with my granddaughters, who used to live in your apartment."

Suddenly, a buzzer sounded and the door unlocked. The group stepped inside the building and walked down the hall to the girls' old apartment. Halfway there, they were greeted by an excited woman with huge red glasses.

"I'm so thrilled to meet you," she said.

"I hope we aren't imposing," Granny Relda said. "We were in the neighborhood."

"Nonsense, I've always wanted to meet the previous owners," the woman said, holding out her hand. "My name is Gloria Frank."

"I'm Relda Grimm. These are my granddaughters, Sabrina and Daphne . . . and Moth."

"Hello, peasant," Moth said, awkwardly hoisting Puck's cocoon onto her shoulder.

Gloria Frank looked confused but smiled. "Please, come in," she said, ushering them down the hall and into the apartment.

For Sabrina, stepping into the living room was a shock. Their once colorful home was now painted in drab shades of wheat. The hardwood floors had been redone, stealing all their old charm and personality, and many of the antique light fixtures had been replaced with austere, modern lamps. All of the furniture Sabrina remembered was gone. Their big puffy couch had been replaced with a sleek chocolate-brown sofa that looked more like a work of art than something to sit on. Every photograph of her family was gone. Even Daphne's finger paintings were no longer hanging on the refrigerator.

Just then, a teenage boy walked out of one of the bedrooms. He was a lanky kid wearing a rugby shirt and carrying a handheld video game. He had curly blond hair and a pair of headphones in his ears. When he saw the visitors, he took off the headphones and regarded the group curiously. "Mom? What is that awful smell?"

"His Majesty's healing vessel gives off an unusual scent but it is not by any means awful," Moth said. "You should be honored to have found its aroma in your nose, you undeserving wretch."

"I'm so sorry," Granny said, stepping between Moth and everyone else. "My granddaughter is in a play and she's been practicing her lines nonstop. Unfortunately, they're using some unusual props and she feels its best to carry one with her."

"She's a method actress. How delightful! My son is an actor, too," Mrs. Frank said as she turned to her son. "What was the last play your school did? You were incredible in it. What was it called?"

"*A Midsummer Night's Dream.*"

"He played Puck. Do you girls know that play?"

"We're living it," Sabrina murmured as the cocoon gave off a particularly noxious blast of gas.

"Phil, these girls used to live here," Mrs. Frank said, waving her hand in front of her nose, and then seeming to realize that this might be rude, pretended to smooth her hair instead.

"Wassup?" the boy said,

"You have my old bedroom," Daphne said, quietly.

Phil raised his eyes and nodded, then put his headphones back on and wandered out of the room.

"I'm sorry. Since we bought him that game we can't get it away from him," his mother said. "Can I take your coats?"

"We can't stay," Granny said. "We just wanted to come by and see who lived here now."

"Oh, we really love the apartment. I hope you think we're taking good care of it," Mrs. Frank said.

Sabrina didn't answer. She kept glancing around the room, trying to find something she recognized. The whole experience was making her dizzy.

"Mrs. Frank, there is one other thing. We were wondering if you happened to find anything in the apartment when you moved in, say, for instance, a journal or a book of stories about fairy-tale characters?" Granny said. "The girls' mother may have kept one and we'd love to get our hands on it."

"Oh, we found a few things when we redid the kitchen and the closets," the woman said. She rushed out of the room and returned with an old shoebox. "My husband told me I was crazy to keep this stuff. He says I'm a pack rat, but they seemed personal and, well, it felt wrong to throw them out."

Sabrina took the box and flipped open the lid. Inside were a few yellowing love letters their father had written their mother, some scattered pictures of Sabrina and Daphne in the bathtub when they were little, and a ladies' wallet with pink roses sewn on the front.

"No journal," Daphne said with a sigh.

"Oh, dear, it's not here," their grandmother said. "Do you think you might have overlooked it?" she said to Mrs. Frank.

Gloria Frank shook her head. "We did a lot of work on this place when we moved in. If there were a journal, we would have found it. I'm sorry."

"Well, we appreciate you hanging onto these things," Granny said. "We should probably be going."

"It was so nice to meet you," Mrs. Frank said. "Don't worry, we'll take good care of this place."

Granny and the girls waited at the bus stop until the next bus came. They climbed inside and found a seat in the back. Moth chattered on about how ignorant human beings could be, but the Grimm women were silent. Sabrina sat by the window, watching her neighborhood disappear.

• • •

Back at the hotel, the little group waited for the elevator. When the doors opened, they were startled to see Mr. Hamstead and Bess inside, locked in a passionate kiss. When the couple finally noticed everyone staring, Hamstead's face went pink and his snout popped out. He quickly put his hand over it, eyeing Bess nervously as if he didn't want her to see. Bess on the other hand was grinning from ear to ear and holding him in her arms like they were lost at sea and he was a life preserver.

"Uh, hello," Granny said as the couple stepped out of the elevator. "Is Mr. Canis awake?"

"Yes," Hamstead said, his face still pink. "He's in his room and wants to speak with you. I asked him if everything was OK and he nearly bit my head off, literally." He blushed even more brightly when he noticed that Daphne was giving him playful winks.

"We just stopped by for some hot cocoa," Bess said. "Wall Street was a bust. It's incredible how fractured our community is. We live such separate, secret lives. We're going to try SoHo and Chinatown next." The blonde lady turned to Hamstead and gave him a big, over-the-top smooch on the cheek. "Sugar dumpling, I'm going to go freshen up. Mind if I borrow your room key?"

"Not at all," Hamstead said. He dug into his pocket and handed the key to her. A moment later, she was back inside the elevator and on her way upstairs.

"Mr. Hamstead, I do believe you are smitten with her," Granny said.

"What does *smitten* mean?" Daphne asked.

Sabrina turned to answer but then noticed something unusual. The little girl was asking Granny Relda instead of her.

"It means he's got a *huge* crush on her," Granny said.

"Which is a *huge* problem," Mr. Hamstead said. "When she finds out who I am . . . what I am—"

"Ernest, she's an Everafter, too, obviously," Granny Relda said.

"A human Everafter," Hamstead said. "I'm a pig. There's a big difference."

"But there are lots of mixed-Everafter couples. You're forgetting Miss Muffet and the spider."

"Miss Muffet is a crackpot," Hamstead said. "Bess is beautiful and funny and the most amazing woman I've ever met. She's not going to be interested in me when she discovers I'm just an unemployed pig from upstate."

Granny smiled. "I'm sure that Bess likes you for who you are."

"If this pointless conversation is over," Moth complained, "I'd like to get His Majesty back to the room."

"Of course," Granny said. "I'm going to pop in on Mr. Canis. I'll meet you soon."

The girls went up to their room and closed the door. Moth climbed onto one of the two queen-sized beds and propped the icky cocoon onto a pillow. "I need silence, humans," she announced.

Sabrina rolled her eyes. "Fine," she said turning to her sister. "I need to talk to you." She gestured to the bathroom and Daphne followed her inside.

"Daphne, Granny and I have talked and we've come to an understanding—"

"I know all about it," Daphne said, stiffly.

"Then you know I'm not going to be involved in this detective stuff anymore."

"I know you're quitting."

"I don't want you to do it, either. We should be trying to find out how to wake Mom and Dad up, anyway. Once they're back to normal, we can move somewhere normal and be a family again. Doesn't that sound good?"

Suddenly Daphne burst into tears. They streamed down her face and onto the shoebox Gloria Frank had given them, which she still clutched in her hands.

"Why are you crying?" Sabrina said, dismayed. "Don't you want to get back to normal?"

"*No!*" Daphne yelled. "This is our destiny."

"You don't even know what the word *destiny* means." For the first time in Sabrina's life, she saw rage in her little sister's eyes. Before Sabrina knew what had happened, Daphne set down the shoebox, opened the door to the shower, turned on the water, and shoved Sabrina inside.

"You little—!" Sabrina sputtered. "I'm trying to protect us."

"No you're not! You're trying to protect yourself. You haven't once asked me what I want. You're a . . . jerkazoid and I don't need you. I'll be a fairy-tale detective all by myself!" Daphne turned and stomped out of the room, slamming the bathroom door behind her.

Soaked to the bone, Sabrina climbed out of the shower, took off her clothes, and put on one of the fancy white robes the hotel had left hanging on the back of the door. She wrapped her head in a towel and thought about what her sister had just said. Daphne was mad, but Sabrina would make her understand. She was doing this for both of them.

The little girl had left the shoebox sitting on the toilet tank. Sabrina picked it up and opened the lid. The photos were the embarrassing bathtub shots that parents love to take and kids wished would be lost in a fire. But they made Sabrina smile. They represented happier times. She flipped through the yellowing love letters, tied in a small red ribbon, and then opened the pink wallet. Inside was her mother's driver's license, some expired credit cards, a couple of pictures of her father, and a photo of Veronica sitting with her daughters. Sabrina and Daphne had their faces painted with stars and rainbows and were smiling. Sabrina remembered that day clearly. Her mother had taken them to a fair held at the South Street Seaport—it had been a good day.

It was odd to hold something her mother had owned. The girls didn't have a single item from their old lives; even their clothes were gone. Sabrina lifted the wallet to her nose and sniffed deeply, hoping to find some hint of her mother's perfume, but all she could smell was old leather.

5

ith her sister not talking to her and Moth shooting her angry looks, Sabrina turned to the book her grandmother had given her when they had arrived in the city. *A Midsummer Night's Dream* was a play, starring Puck and his obnoxious parents. Cobweb and Moth were in it as well. Though the old-fashioned writing was challenging, it didn't take a brain surgeon to realize Shakespeare had his hands full with Oberon and Titania. He described them both as petty, jealous, and manipulative. Apparently, Sabrina realized, nothing had changed in the four hundred plus years since the play had been written.

When Granny returned to the room, Mr. Canis was with her. Except for a glimpse that morning, Sabrina hadn't seen him since the night before. She was shocked at his appearance. He had grown several inches in height and packed on twenty pounds of muscle. His shock of white hair now had brown streaks in it and he had what looked like the definite beginnings of a beard and mustache. Sabrina knew what was happening to the old man. Lately, whenever he tapped into the Big Bad Wolf's power, he lost a little more of himself. She wondered what the family would do when there was no more of Mr. Canis to lose, but she said nothing. Granny didn't mention anything either, and acted as if all was well. She was eager to get back on the case and urged the girls to hurry and put on their coats, hats, and mittens.

Most of the day was spent scurrying from one neighborhood to the next, hoping beyond hope that they would stumble upon an Everafter. Bess had given them plenty of leads but all had been dead ends. Still, Granny Relda was determined. She must have poked her head into every dark restaurant and creepy alley in Manhattan. They spoke to dozens of street people, who knew more neighborhood secrets than anyone else. Many were homeless, and Granny Relda thanked them all for their time and information with five-dollar bills, insisting they use the money to put something warm in their bellies. But none of their tips led the family to Everafters. The closest the detectives got was discovering a man wearing a wedding dress riding a multicolored bicycle around Washington Square Park. He turned out to be human.

With Mr. Hamstead and Bess no doubt sharing a romantic meal somewhere, the rest of the investigators decided to stop for an early dinner at a small Chinese restaurant called the Happy Duck. As they went inside, Sabrina noticed eight roasted ducks hanging in the window and wondered if they were all that happy.

The restaurant was the kind of place where the menu was as big as a phone book, the staff spoke little English, and the tables were crowded together. The waiters eyed Puck's cocoon and pinched their noses in disgust as the group made their way to a table in the back near a huge fish tank. Daphne ordered for the whole table, and enough food for several others, and Sabrina relaxed, thinking the meal would be a welcome, cheering break from tramping through the snow. But Granny snuck off to make a phone call halfway through the feast; Mr. Canis sat silently throughout with his eyes closed, breathing in and out in a slow pattern; Puck's cocoon kept rubbing up against Sabrina, drenching her in sticky goo; Daphne was still not talking to her; and Moth refused to eat, saying the food was a travesty and unfit for pigs. It was the most uncomfortable meal of Sabrina's entire life. She couldn't have been more relieved when her grandmother returned to the table.

"Your Uncle Jacob says everything is well," Granny said.

"Has he found a way to wake up Mom and Dad?" Sabrina asked, hopefully.

Granny shook her head. "He said he was trying every magical potion we have in the house. Unfortunately, he's had to abandon the place for a couple of days."

"Why? What happened?"

"He made the mistake of giving Elvis a plate of sausage."

Giving their dog Elvis sausage was a big no-no. It did bad things to the two-hundred-pound Great Dane. Very bad, very smelly things. The last time Daphne had given him sausage they'd almost had to move.

"I miss Elvis," the little girl said. She leaned back in her chair and rubbed her protruding belly. "Look at me. I'm having a baby. I'm going to name him Number 15 with Egg Roll."

Granny laughed. "*Liebling,* you've got food all down the front of your shirt. Let me take you into the bathroom and clean you up."

Daphne shrugged as if she didn't care but followed the old woman anyway.

"I believe I would like to wash my hands," Mr. Canis said, and got up as well. Unfortunately, that left Sabrina and Moth alone. Sabrina tried to ignore the fairy girl but Moth's angry eyes were boring into her.

"Let's make something clear, human," Moth said. "If you attempt to interfere in my relationship with Puck you will regret it. He is my fiancée!"

"Listen, I don't want your fiancée. I'm eleven. I'm not even allowed to have a boyfriend, so when Puck finally crawls out of his icky ball you can be sure he's all yours."

"You do not love him?" Moth said.

"NO!" Sabrina said a little too loudly. She looked around the room and felt every eye on her, including those of Mr. Canis, who was waiting in line for the bathroom. He had a smile on his face, but when she shot him an angry look it disappeared, and he went back to studying the ceiling.

"I do not want anything to confuse Puck when he finally reconsiders Oberon's choice," Moth said.

"What are you talking about? What is Oberon's choice?"

"*Me,* I am Oberon's choice. He selected me to be Puck's bride," Moth said.

"What do you mean he selected you?"

"It's called the father's privilege. Fairy fathers choose their son's mates."

"Oh, I bet Puck loved that! I wish I could have seen his face when his dad made that announcement!"

Moth snarled, and Sabrina realized the girl took the subject very seriously.

"So then what happened?" Sabrina asked.

"The prince was confused . . ."

"You mean he dumped you," Sabrina said.

"He *made* a mistake and, unfortunately, his father punished him for it. Puck was banished from Faerie. That was more than ten years ago and we hadn't heard from him . . . until yesterday," Moth said.

"He's been stuck in Ferryport Landing. It's like a big roach motel. You can check in but you can't check out," Sabrina said. "From what I know of him you shouldn't be too upset he left. Puck would drive you crazy. You're better off without him."

"How dare you!" Moth cried. "King Puck is a great fairy."

"Sorry," Sabrina said. "But I have to ask you, if he left town to avoid getting married once, why do you think things are going to be different this time?"

Moth snarled but said nothing.

"Well, I hope it works out for you," Sabrina said sarcastically. "The Trickster King is a real catch."

The two girls sat in silence until the others returned to the table.

"Who wants some lychee ice cream?" Daphne cried.

"You're still hungry?" Mr. Canis asked.

"I'm still awake, aren't I?"

While everyone looked over the dessert menu, Sabrina took her mother's little pink wallet out of her pocket and flipped it open. She stole a peek at her mom's picture. Just then she noticed a small flap hidden behind the photo. She opened it, stuck her fingers inside, and pulled out an oddly colored business card. It was dark blue and covered in little moons and stars and had an inscription:

Scrooge's Financial and Spiritual Advice
Affordable Rates!
18 West 18th Street
Voted Best Psychic by Time Out New York *Magazine*

Sabrina flipped the card over and discovered handwriting on the other side.

Veronica, stop by anytime. I owe you one!
E. Scrooge

"What did you find?" Granny Relda asked.

"Just some old business card in my mother's wallet," Sabrina said, handing it over. "I think it's for a psychic or something."

Granny read the inscription and a big grin filled her face. "Sabrina, for someone who doesn't want to be a detective you're very good at it. You just found an important clue!"

Sabrina was dumbfounded. "Clue? It's just a card for some scam artist."

"Maybe, maybe not," the old woman said, waving the card like it was a winning lottery ticket. "But whether he's the real deal doesn't matter. What's important is that he's an Everafter and we've got his address!"

Daphne took the card and read the inscription. "What makes you think he's an Everafter?"

"Look at the name on the card—E. Scrooge!"

"Yeah, so?" Sabrina said.

"E. Scrooge . . . as in Ebenezer Scrooge," Granny said.

"The guy from *A Christmas Carol?*" Daphne said as she prepared her palm for biting.

"The one and only," Granny said.

Daphne bit down hard.

• • •

Eighteenth Street was a pothole-riddled road in a part of town called Chelsea. As the group made their way to Scrooge's shop, they passed an art supply store, a vintage record outlet, a children's bookstore, and several places where a person could buy mannequins and sewing machine parts. Scrooge's Financial and Spiritual Advice was in the middle of the block. In the grimy window was an enormous green-neon sign with an eye that blinked every few moments below the words SPIRITS AND SAVINGS BONDS.

Sabrina studied the sign for a moment, running through everything she knew about Scrooge in her mind. Charles Dickens had documented the story: A greedy businessman was visited by the ghosts of Christmas. She had seen the musical at Madison Square Garden when she was little and clearly remembered Scrooge as a nasty old man.

The waiting room was crowded with some of the strangest people Sabrina had ever seen. They wore what could only be called holiday-themed costumes, from every holiday imaginable—patriotic uniforms with sparklers, bright emerald suits covered in shamrocks, turkey costumes, cupid outfits—there was even a guy wearing a big paper top hat and a pair of glasses that read HAPPY NEW YEAR!

The family approached an empty desk at the far end of the room. A little sign on top read TIM CRATCHIT. Next to it was a silver bell with another sign that read RING BELL FOR SERVICE. Granny tapped it lightly, sending a chiming sound into the air.

"I'll be right out!" a voice shouted from behind a closed door near the desk. The voice was followed by a mechanical sound, like an engine, and another noise, like something heavy had crashed into a box of fine china. Moments later, a kid with a round face and freckles appeared in the doorway on a motorized chair. He seemed to have no control over the machine and he repeatedly slammed it into the doorframe. After several minutes of labored backing up, and then failed efforts to roll forward, he finally got the chair through the narrow doorway. Unfortunately, his problems didn't stop there. Once he entered the room, he slammed the chair into the desk and sent it crashing to the floor.

"Blast it!" the kid shouted in a thick English accent. He tried to pull the desk upright and nearly tipped himself onto the floor in the process. Exhausted just from watching him, Sabrina stepped in and lifted the desk upright. Once the boy was comfortably situated, the waiting room crowd rushed forward, jostling the investigators to the back of the line. Everyone began arguing at once.

"I have to be somewhere in fifteen minutes," said the man wearing New Year's glasses. He took a small plastic horn out of his mouth and gave it an angry toot.

"Well, I was here first," a giant complained as he pushed himself to the front. He was covered in leaves and pinecones and smelled like a forest.

Tim Cratchit whistled loudly and the crowd grew silent. "Are any of you paying customers?"

"C'mon, Tim!" an enormous man in a bunny suit said. "We've been waiting all day."

"And you'll wait all night!" Tim cried. "You buggers show up anytime you please. Mr. Scrooge is a busy man and hasn't the time to waste on a bunch of penniless layabouts."

"Uh, we've got money," Granny said.

Tim's eyes searched for her in the crowd and then he smiled. "Are you alive?"

Sabrina and Daphne eyed each other.

"Last time I checked," Sabrina said.

"Well, I can't just take your word for it," Tim said as he accidentally pushed a button that sent the chair slamming into the desk again. "We're very busy here and we only have time for *paying and living* customers."

His words caused the crowd to erupt in protest.

"You want proof that we're alive?" Mr. Canis asked as he and the others approached the desk. "How do we do that?"

The boy reached over to Sabrina and Daphne and gave them both painful pinches on the arm. They yelped angrily and Daphne kicked the boy's chair.

"OK, I'm satisfied. Now, are you here for the boss's financial expertise or are you interested in his supernatural skills?"

"I'm not really sure," Granny said. "We want to ask him a few questions."

"Well, have a seat and I'll see if he can fit you in," Tim said as he began the laborious effort of turning his mechanical chair around and steering it back through the door from which he had come. When he disappeared through it, there were more loud crashes and then shouts from another, angry voice.

"Tim Cratchit! Do you have any idea how much a box of crystal balls costs these days? I didn't buy you that mechanical chair so you could race through the store trashing everything."

"Sorry, boss," Tim shouted. "You've got customers . . . and they're breathers!"

Suddenly, the door flew open and a thin, wiry old man in a black suit hurried into the room. His hair was bushy and white and stood up in all directions, almost as if he had been repeatedly scared out of his wits.

"So, who was next?" he said with a broad smile.

Everyone in the waiting room said, "Me!"

"Only the living people, people!" Scrooge bellowed.

"That would be us," Granny said, taking the opportunity to usher the girls and Mr. Canis forward.

"Excellent," the old man said as he gestured for the group to follow him into the back. They had to wait for Tim to get out of the doorway, but once this was accomplished, they found themselves in a room decorated in ruby and midnight-blue tapestries with fluffy pillows scattered on the floor. Incense burned in a small pot on a shelf. In the middle of the room was a round table surrounded by six high-backed chairs. The old man invited everyone to sit down and then did so himself.

"I apologize for that mob scene. I hired Tim to keep them out but I think the boy is in over his head," he continued. "Ghosts can be quite a handful."

"Ghosts!" Sabrina said with a laugh.

If the man heard the doubt in her voice he ignored it. "They're like mice. I can't get rid of them. Ever since that business with the Ghosts of Christmas Past, Present, and Future, all the spirits in the astral plane feel it's their duty to come and show me how I've ruined the holidays of everyone I know. I'll admit, I was a pain at Christmastime, but since then I've been haunted by the Ghosts of Easter, Passover, Thanksgiving, Yom Kippur, the anniversary of the Boxer Rebellion, Bastille Day, Lincoln's Birthday; anything you can think of! The whole thing has gotten ridiculous. How many Arbor Days could I have ruined? Not to mention Kwanzaa, Secretary's Day, and the anniversary of the Woodstock concert. It got so bad I was fired from my job at the bank. It's really difficult to approve home loans with the Ghost of Earth Day Future walking around turning off all the office computers to save energy."

Scrooge bent under the table and came up with a calculator and a crystal ball. "OK, let's get down to business. We do two things here: finances and phantoms. What's it going to be?"

Granny reached into her handbag and removed the business card Sabrina had found in her mother's wallet. Scrooge took it, flipped it over, and then smiled.

"Ah, Veronica," he said, wistfully. "Where did you get this?"

"She's my mom," Daphne said.

The man grinned. "Your mother is a saint. She helped me get the lease on this store when I decided to go into business for myself. She's lovely. Just lovely! What can I do for you?"

"We're investigating King Oberon's death and we were hoping you might—"

"Of course!" Scrooge said, cutting off Granny Relda. "Everybody grab hands and close your eyes."

"Mr. Scrooge, I'm a bit confused. We aren't here to talk to spirits," the old woman said.

"Oh."

"We were hoping you might be able to give us some information. Anything you might know about who would've wanted to kill the king."

Scrooge laughed. "Well, you don't need a psychic for that. Everyone wanted to kill the king. I wanted to kill the king. He was a jerk!"

"—azoid," Daphne finished.

"He was arrogant, stupid, meddling," Scrooge cried. "He'd send his goons down here to collect his tax—extortion money if you ask me. Most of us thought he was a royal pain in the—"

"You weren't at the meeting yesterday," Mr. Canis interrupted.

"No, I gave up on all that nonsense when the real Faerie fell," Scrooge said.

"Yes, we keep hearing about Faerie," Sabrina said.

"Faerie was a great idea, a neighborhood of Everafters. It used to be downtown but people started moving in and Everafters kept getting moved out. Pretty soon, we were way out in Jersey City, New Jersey. Well, I wasn't going to tolerate that! An Everafter has got to have standards. Before I knew it we were pushed out of Jersey, too. Eventually, someone suggested the park. No one lives there but the squirrels. They had a witch set up the Golden Egg. Oberon said we'd buy land and start anew, but it never happened.

We couldn't get along long enough to make anything work. But if you want to know about stuff like this you should take it right from the horse's mouth—Oberon himself."

"Old man, did we not just tell you the king is dead?" Mr. Canis snapped.

"You read the sign on the door, right? You people aren't getting it, are you? Here, take my hand," Scrooge said, snatching Sabrina's in his own. "Now, close your eyes. We have to concentrate to get Oberon's attention."

"Is this going to give me nightmares?" Daphne cried, taking Scrooge's other hand.

"Depends . . . was his head chopped off or anything like that? They often come back looking the way they did when they died."

"He was poisoned," Granny Relda said, sounding a little uneasy.

"Should be OK. He might be a little green. Still, I have to warn you. Even if we see Oberon he'll be difficult to understand. I think it has something to do with the energy they use to become full-torso apparitions. They trade the body for the language but we'll do our best—sometimes I can make out what they want to say by having them play charades. Now, let's concentrate. Oberon? Oberon, are you there?"

Sabrina rolled her eyes. "You're just going to call out his name? It's that easy?"

"Fine, if you want the whole shebang there's no extra charge," Scrooge said as he flipped a switch on the wall. Rays of light shot out of the crystal ball, speckling the tapestries with shimmering suns, moons, and stars. The sound of a powerful wind came from speakers mounted on the ceiling. Scrooge reached under the table and pulled out a huge swami hat. It was bright purple and had a shiny red ruby in its center. He plopped it on his head. "This authentic enough for you?"

Sabrina scowled.

"Oberon, King of the Fairies. We call on you. Come forth and reveal yourself," Scrooge continued. Unfortunately, his request went unanswered and the family sat waiting for several minutes.

"I'm sorry. Dead people can be a bit shy," the psychic said nervously. His former confidence seemed to fade. "Oberon, come out, come out wherever you are. That's right, Your Majesty, we're having a party and you're invited."

"This is ridiculous," Sabrina said, leaping to her feet. She was fully prepared to march out of the room when an odd chill crept up her spine. She felt as if she had a horrible head cold. In fact, her whole body felt weird, almost as if it were filled with stuffing, like she had become a giant teddy bear.

"Granny, what's going on?" Sabrina cried as she watched the hair on her arms stand on end.

"I think he's here," Scrooge said, sounding relieved. "Oberon, is that you?"

Sabrina's mouth opened on its own and a ghostly voice echoed out of it. "Where am I?"

"Hey! Did that come out of me?" Sabrina cried, looking at her sister, who stared at her with eyes as wide as moons. Even Moth looked a bit freaked out.

"Wowzers!" Scrooge said to Sabrina. "You're a natural medium. Ghosts feel comfortable talking through you. Your mother had the same ability!"

But Sabrina couldn't respond. The ghost had full possession of her now. "Where am I?" the voice said. This time Sabrina's arms flailed around as if she were angry.

Scrooge bit his lip. "Oberon, I have some bad news for you. Are you sitting down?"

"I don't know," Oberon's voice said. "Hey! Where's my body?"

"Yeah, that's the bad news. You're dead."

There was a long silence but Sabrina could still feel the king's presence inside of her. Suddenly, her mouth opened again and a single frustrated word came out.

"Fudge."

"I know. It's a real bummer. Right now, you're stuck in limbo and you're going to stay there until your killer is brought to justice. Luckily, we've got some people here who want to help you out with that inconvenience."

"King Oberon, it is I, your loyal subject, Moth. I have been caring for Puck since you have departed," the little fairy bragged as she hefted Puck's cocoon onto the table. "He is here with me."

"I know, I can smell him from the astral plane," Oberon groaned, then forced Sabrina's body to walk over to Puck's cocoon. Sabrina felt her hand move over it, caressing the cocoon lightly. She could feel a wave of regret pour over her, an odd sensation considering how Oberon reacted when he discovered Puck in his office. Hadn't he called his son a traitor? Sabrina also felt Oberon's hold on her body weaken. She took the opportunity to wrench back control.

"Get out of me!" she demanded.

"Sabrina, don't fight him. We need to ask him some important questions," Granny said.

"Easy for you to say. There's only one person in your body," Sabrina cried.

"Oberon, do you have any idea who killed you?" Granny Relda said.

"*Cobweb!*" the voice bellowed as Oberon took control again. "He poisoned me. He brought me a glass of wine to celebrate the arrival of Veronica's girls. A moment after he left I felt faint and collapsed. Then there was a terrible pain and blackness."

"I knew it!" Moth cried.

The family looked at her in disbelief.

"Well, I did!"

"Do you know why he wanted to kill you?" Granny asked Oberon.

"No," the king said. "He's the last person I would have suspected. Oh, I am so angry! I had Rangers tickets this season. What a waste!"

"Are you sure Cobweb acted alone?" Mr. Canis said. "Perhaps he was working with another person who wanted you dead."

"Like who? Everyone loves me!"

"We saw you fighting with your wife," Granny replied.

"Titania? Impossible! She wouldn't kill me. Sure we fight, but you try being married for five thousand years and see if you don't bicker."

"Did you know that Cobweb was a member of the Scarlet Hand?" Granny asked.

"The Scarlet what?" Oberon asked. "I've never heard of any Scarlet Hand. Listen, you've got to find Cobweb and bring him to justice."

Suddenly, the chill in Sabrina's body disappeared and a new voice came from her mouth. "Please insert fifty cents for ten more minutes."

"Sorry, we've lost the connection," Scrooge said.

"Well, get him back!" Moth cried. "We need to know if Oberon suspects anyone else!"

"I'm sorry. He's gone. I hope it was helpful," Scrooge said.

Granny stood up. "It was more than helpful. We now know who killed Oberon and all we have to do is track down this Cobweb. If only detective work were always this easy."

"Forget detective work," Scrooge said. "Sabrina could make a bundle as a psychic."

Sabrina cringed.

The group thanked Scrooge for his help and then exited the room, where they found Tim struggling with his desk, again. They helped him set it upright and then paid Scrooge's fee.

"Satisfied customers, eh? Well, well, that's good news," Tim said as he counted the bills. "The guvnor tends to get a lot of bad connections these days. I was a big fan of your mother, by the way. She was good people."

Daphne rested her elbows on his desk and smiled brightly. "Would you say it for me?" she asked.

"Say what?"

"You know! The line," the little girl begged.

Tim frowned, rolled his eyes, and took a deep breath. "God Bless Us, Every One," he grumbled.

Daphne clapped her hands and giggled like she'd just stumbled into a surprise party.

"I should start charging for that," Tim muttered.

"So we know who killed Oberon. What do we do now?" Sabrina said when the group stepped back out into the street.

"Mustardseed said to report everything to Oz," Granny said as she raised her hand to hail a cab. One quickly pulled over.

"Where to, folks?" the cabbie said.

"Macy's department store," Granny said, as she helped the girls into the taxi.

"I'm feeling tired," Mr. Canis said from the sidewalk. "I believe I could use some time alone. Do you think you can manage without me?"

Granny nodded. "Do you need a ride?"

Mr. Canis shook his head. Relda waved good-bye, and the taxi pulled away from the curb and headed north toward Macy's.

Daphne clapped her hands. "We're off to see the Wizard."

Sabrina rolled her eyes. "You've been waiting all day to say that, haven't you?"

Daphne grinned from ear to ear.

• • •

When they arrived at Macy's, they found a huge crowd of people pushing their way into the store at the same time that an equally huge crowd was trying to get out. Sabrina was not surprised. After all, Christmas Eve was just three days away and what would the holidays be without thousands of panicked shoppers scrambling for last-minute gifts? Granny urged them all to hold hands as they politely moved through the mob.

"Mommy!" a small child cried as he pointed at Puck's cocoon. "I want that for Christmas!"

Sabrina snickered to herself, imagining the stinky sac underneath a Christmas tree. She would love to see Puck's face when he crawled out of it only to find a weird little boy staring at him.

"So, did Oz say what he does at the store?" Daphne yelled above the crowd.

"No, but I'm sure if we ask, someone will help us find him," Granny Relda said. "He's a bit of a character. Everyone must know him."

"I found him," Moth said, pointing at one of the many huge picture windows that ran along the sides of the block-long building at Herald Square. There was Oz behind the glass, working on a window display featuring several elves who were supposed to be assembling toys in a red-and-green factory. The elves were robots, run by electricity, yet they moved like human beings, laughing, waving, and pounding away on their toys. One, however, had obviously gone haywire. It was pounding on its robot brethren. Oz stood nearby, aiming his silver remote at the malfunctioning elf. A throng of people pressed against the window, watching the wizard work on the remarkable creations and giggling at his troubles. Sabrina glanced down the street and noticed that there were similar crowds ogling the other windows, which featured scenes from *The Night Before Christmas, A Christmas Carol,* and *The Nutcracker.* Each window display was more magical than the last. Sabrina remembered that L. Frank Baum, the man who had written about the land of Oz, had described the Wizard as a mechanical genius, able to create realistic, even frightening illusions. He was so talented, he had once convinced the entire country of Oz that he was a powerful sorcerer.

Granny maneuvered through the crowd and tapped on the window. Oz turned with an irritated expression, which disappeared when he spotted her. He waved for her to come inside and then climbed out of the back of the window display.

The group squirmed their way into the bustling store, where Oz met them. He shook their hands and then ushered them into a room marked STAFF ONLY. What Sabrina saw inside was even more amazing than the window displays. The room was filled with half-finished figures, many blinking and buzzing, waiting for their moment in the spotlight. Robotic birds sat on perches singing sweet little songs, and a family of half-painted polar bears played with a newborn cub in the corner. They looked so real it was hard not to get nervous around them. There were also stacks of papers and old engineering books lying about, a full-length mirror leaning against the wall, and a cot sitting in the far corner. Sabrina suspected the Wizard slept in his workroom more often than not.

"I'm sorry I'm so frazzled," Oz said as he offered everyone a seat. "Today is 'what-happened-to-the-rest-of-the-year?' day here at the store. You'd think people might realize there are three hundred sixty-four days to shop before Christmas."

"We were admiring your windows," Granny said. "The displays are extraordinary."

Oz picked up a robot head. It blinked at him and smiled. "Yes, well, it's the closest thing I'll get to real magic. I used to be a first rate slight-of-hand man back in the day. When I first found myself in Oz, I did a trick for the Mayor of Munchkinland and before I knew it, I was the Great and Terrible Oz! Unfortunately, there isn't a lot of demand in New York City for a guy with that title. I tried my hand entertaining at kids' birthday parties, but video games put an end to that, of course. When I heard about this job, I jumped at it. I always had a knack for mechanical things. Now I create illusions with circuits instead of my hands."

"They look almost real," Daphne said.

"Thank you," Oz replied. "They're like my children. In fact, if I can't get that elf in the window to behave I'm going to have to put him in time-out. Now, I know you all didn't come down here just to admire the decorations. How goes the search?"

"We've got a suspect," Daphne said.

Oz raised an eyebrow.

"Cobweb," Granny said.

"That can't be," Oz said.

"Oberon told us," Daphne added.

The Wizard raised both eyebrows.

"It's a long story," Granny said. "We believe Cobweb's been working with a group called the Scarlet Hand."

"That mark they found on Oberon," Oz said.

Granny nodded. "Can you pass this information on to Mustardseed? He may be in danger from Cobweb, as well."

"Of course," Oz said.

"Unfortunately, that brings us to another dead end. We don't know where to find Cobweb. He's not still at the Golden Egg, is he?"

"No, all but Titania, Mustardseed, and his men have scattered."

"Did he have any friends?" Granny Relda asked.

The Wizard shook his head. "He was pretty busy following Oberon and Titania's orders. He was very loyal to them. That's what makes this all such a big surprise. Still, there might be someone who can help. There's a fairy godmother over in west Midtown who I've seen with Cobweb. If he needs a place to hide, he might head there. Her name is Twilarose. She owns a dress shop."

"That's a big help," Daphne said.

"By the way," Oz said. "Between me and you, your friend, the chubby guy . . ."

"Mr. Hamstead?" Sabrina asked.

"Yes. He's made himself a powerful enemy today. Word is he stole Tony Fats's girlfriend. If I were him, I'd get out of town as fast as possible. The fairy godfathers aren't people you mess around with."

• • •

Twilarose's Fashion Emporium was on the corner of Eleventh Avenue and Fifty-seventh Street next to a parking lot for garbage trucks. The smell on the block was even worse than the one coming from Puck's cocoon.

Granny had left word at the hotel for Mr. Hamstead and Bess

to meet them at the fairy godmother's store. They arrived soon after the Grimms and Moth, though they were so caught up in conversation, they barely noticed the family waiting for them in the fading daylight. Granny pulled the couple aside and gave them Oz's warning. Bess looked concerned but Mr. Hamstead just smiled and reminded Granny Relda that he was more than capable of taking care of himself and Bess, if need be.

While the grown-ups talked, Sabrina looked at the store's window display and decided that this Twilarose person wasn't exactly sure what the word *fashion* meant. The dresses were so ruffled and brightly colored that the mannequins wearing them looked embarrassed.

"So what's the difference between a fairy and a fairy god-mother?" Daphne asked Moth.

The little fairy sneered. "Of course an ignoramus like you wouldn't know the difference. Fairy godmothers and godfathers are lower beings. Unlike true-blood fairies, they need wands to perform magic. And they are born as adults, sometimes as very old people. They can be painfully ugly, with their gray hair and wrinkles."

"It must take great strength on your part to tolerate them," said Granny Relda, who had caught the end of Moth's speech.

"It does," Moth said, nodding earnestly.

"Well, we don't know this Twilarose and if she's hiding Cobweb she might be dangerous," Hamstead said, pulling his pants up over his belly. "Be careful and keep your eyes peeled."

A fat, orange tomcat lay outside, blocking the entrance to the store. Granny shooed it away and it raced shrieking into an old refrigerator box someone had dragged out onto the sidewalk.

Inside the shop, they found racks and racks of shiny, poofy-sleeved ballroom dresses, covered in frills and lace. There were also several shelves of shoes in shocking, unnatural colors and funky-shaped handbags.

A roly-poly lady stepped out of the back room and approached the group. She had a big, blue beehive hairdo atop an almost perfect circle of a head. Her eyebrows were drawn on and her cheeks and lips were bright pink. She was wearing a baby-blue satin dress that made it look as if she might be off to her senior prom at any moment. A rhinestone belt with blue-and-green blinking lights completed the look.

"Welcome to Twilarose's Fashion Emporium. How can I help you?" the woman sang. "We're having a sale on spring-fling formal wear and shoes. It's never too early to get a head start on the coming seasons. And remember, everything in this store is a Twilarose original. I design everything myself."

"So you're Twilarose?" Granny asked.

"The one and only," the old woman said. "Perhaps you've seen my work on the runways of Milan, Paris, and Canton, Ohio."

"The Wizard of Oz sent us," Daphne said.

"We're looking for Cobweb," Granny Relda added.

Twilarose's eyes grew wide. "Indeed. Oh my! I didn't recognize you, the *Grimm family*," she said louder than necessary. "I'm so glad none of you people in the *Grimm family* were hurt in that mob scene at the Golden Egg. Terrible, terrible situation. I'm so thrilled to meet the *Grimm family*."

"Well, I guess we know he's here somewhere," Sabrina said. The woman was obviously trying to warn Cobweb of their arrival.

"I'm not sure what you're talking about, you people in the *Grimm family!* I just make clothing. In fact, I feel inspired. I'm going to give you all the Twilarose VIP Makeover! Won't that be fun?"

Twilarose reached into the folds of her dress and produced a magic wand. She waved it in the air and there was a loud *bam!* When Sabrina looked down, she was wearing a puffy, leopard-print dress with matching shoes. She looked over at the others and saw their clothes had been replaced as well. Daphne had on a rainbow-colored can-can dress and Granny Relda was wearing a big pink gown with a hat as large as her whole body. Moth and Bess were both dressed in tracksuits covered in little golden bells and had snowshoes on their feet. Each of the women had so much makeup on, it looked as if it had been applied with a paint-ball gun.

Poor Mr. Hamstead was wearing an electric-blue tuxedo with tails and a top hat. Even Puck's cocoon had been made over, in different colored ribbons.

Twilarose clapped her hands. "I am brilliant!" she shouted. "You all are going to be the toast of New York City."

"Underling, we don't have time for this nonsense," Moth said.

"Oh no! You don't like the outfits. Maybe something more work-appropriate? I'll fix you lickety-split!" The fairy god-mother waved her wand again and *bam!*—the dresses were gone, replaced with outfits that were even more outrageous. Now, each of the women was wearing a long evening gown that had a badge, handcuffs, and a billy club swinging from it. Mr. Hamstead was dressed in a black-and-white prison uniform and had a ball and chain around his left leg. He looked down and grunted.

"Genius!" Twilarose said, and then shook her head. "But the makeup is all wrong."

Bam!

Sabrina turned to the mirror. She looked like a geisha from outer space with white pancake makeup and silver lipstick.

Bam!

Now she was wearing fake vampire teeth and a beanie cap with a propeller on top.

Bam!

Sabrina looked down to find she was carrying a toy poodle with a diamond collar, and she herself had two purple shiners and some of her teeth had been blackened out.

"No, maybe it's the shoes," Twilarose said.

Moth stepped forward and waved an angry finger at Twilarose. "I am a fairy and a member of the royal court, making me your superior, so if you are quite finished with your atrocious fashion show—"

"Atrocious?" Twilarose cried. She flicked her wrists and before anyone could stop her, they were all bound from head to toe in thick steel chains.

"It has been a long time since the glory days of Cinderella but I'd hardly call my work atrocious."

"Whoa, whoa, whoa!" Daphne cried. "You're Cinderella's fairy godmother?" She tried to free her hand so she could insert it in her mouth.

"Yes, she's what made me a fashion design icon. After that

dress every princess from here to Timbuktu would have killed for one of my designs . . . but those were the good old days," she said sadly.

"Enough!" Moth roared as she wiggled out of the chains that bound her. "Your blabbering is wasting our time. If you don't tell us where Cobweb is I'll—"

"There is no need for threats, Princess," a voice said from behind the curtains at the back of the store. The drapes were pulled aside and Cobweb stepped through.

"Murderer," Moth screamed.

"You are confused," Cobweb said. "I have killed no one!"

"We know you did it!" Sabrina said. "We heard it straight from Oberon."

"I am innocent," Cobweb said, slightly confused.

Just then, there was a tremendous crash and the front door to the shop blew off its hinges. The group struggled to see what had caused the commotion. Standing in the doorway were Tony Fats and Bobby Screwball. Their magic wands were held tight in their huge hands.

"How did you find us?" Bess cried.

The two goons ignored her. Their eyes were trained on Mr. Hamstead.

"You shouldn't have messed with my girl," Tony Fats said as

he and his partner stepped into the store. "'Cause now, you and me . . . we're going to have to settle this the way we did back in Faerie."

Tony Fats raised his wand and, with a flick of his wrist, a bolt of white-hot energy rocketed toward the group.

6

amstead leaped out of the way and the blast missed him by inches. Unfortunately, it crashed into a rack of polyester dresses that exploded into flames.

"My spring collection!" Twilarose shouted as she desperately tried to put out the fire that was melting her gowns. She stomped feverishly on a pink, hoop-skirted prom dress, completely ignoring the peril of everyone around her.

In the chaos, Sabrina watched Mustardseed fly out of the shop.

"Forget the dresses!" she cried, as flames rapidly spread throughout the store. "Get us out of these chains."

Twilarose turned and flicked her wand. The chains vanished, freeing the group. Unfortunately, smoke was filling the room, and Tony Fats and Bobby Screwball, who seemed to be having trouble seeing, were shooting their wands in every direction. Bobby seemed to have particularly bad aim; each blast from his wand spiraled toward a random target.

"Now I know why they call him Bobby Screwball," Sabrina said as she rushed to rescue Puck's cocoon from a nest of smoldering feather boas. She scampered over to her family, who were hiding behind a rack of capes.

"Where's Cobweb?" Daphne cried.

"He got away," Sabrina said, ducking her head to avoid a blast. "We need to get out of here, too!"

"*Bess!*" Tony Fats bellowed as he fired again. "You're my girl now and always."

"They're blinded by the smoke! They aren't expecting any of us to fly out," Sabrina said, handing Moth Puck's cocoon. "Get him out of here."

"My pleasure," the fairy girl said as her wings sprang from her back and lifted her off the ground. She zipped in between the fairy godfathers' wand blasts and soared out the open door to safety. With so much smoke in the air, Tony and Bobby hadn't even noticed Moth fly by.

"Ernie, take my hand," Bess said. She reached behind her back, pushed something on her backpack, and suddenly a flame shot out that lifted her and her chubby new boyfriend right off the ground. Sabrina was stunned as she watched them rocket out of the store.

"Uh, I want one of those," Daphne said.

Twilarose hurried out next, stumbling over a stack of tiaras before making it to the door.

"Our turn!" Sabrina cried. She snatched Daphne and Granny by the hand and raced across the room. By this time, Bobby and Tony seemed to have gotten wise to what was going on. Their shots came more quickly and the Grimms had to race at full speed to get to the exit. But just as they reached the door, Daphne pulled away and raced back the way they had come, scooping something off the floor and then rejoining her family.

They tumbled out into the street, gasping for air, while Tony and Bobby continued to fire their wands obliviously inside the store. It was amazing they didn't hit each other.

Sabrina rubbed the soot out of her eyes and scanned her surroundings. Twilarose was gone, but Sabrina spied Cobweb flying down the street. "There he is!"

"We'll never catch him on foot," Granny said, whirling around in search of a taxi. She knocked into a woman carrying grocery bags.

"Did you see that?" the woman cried, staring down the street at Cobweb. "That man is flying, like an angel."

Granny nodded, reached into her handbag, and then blew forgetful dust all over the woman. Her eyes glazed over.

"You had a very boring day," Granny said.

"I did," the woman replied.

"Wait a minute!" Daphne cried. She reached up and felt around in the woman's grocery bag.

"What are you doing?" Sabrina asked, eyeing the doorway nervously. Bobby and Tony weren't going to stay in the store forever.

"I need something . . . like a pumpkin," the little girl explained, then yanked out a long green zucchini. "I hope this is close enough."

Sabrina watched Daphne place the zucchini on the ground and then take a long, thin piece of wood out of her pocket—it was Twilarose's magic wand.

"She dropped this," the little girl explained.

"*Liebling,* you have no idea how to use that," Granny said.

"I watched her. It's all in the wrist," Daphne said.

Daphne flicked her wrist and a bolt of energy shot out of the wand and hit the zucchini. There was a blinding flash and when Sabrina's eyes adjusted, she looked down. The zucchini was still there.

Daphne shook the wand vigorously. "I think it needs new batteries."

But in seconds the zucchini began to change. It grew in size and shape, morphing and twisting, creating wheels, hubcaps, headlights, and more. When the transformation was complete, the investigators were standing in front of an emerald-green car, complete with sunroof, spoiler, and whitewall tires.

"This is incredible," Granny Relda said.

"And it goes nicely in a salad," Daphne said, grinning. Then she glanced around and spotted the orange tomcat hovering in the doorway. "Now we need a driver."

She waved the wand again and a blast hit the cat. It let out a surprised shriek and then, just like the zucchini, began to change its shape. In no time at all, the tabby had become a young, red-headed man wearing a black suit and a little leather cap.

"What's your name?" Daphne said.

"Chester," the driver said.

"We need you to follow a flying fairy," Granny said.

"Now there's a sentence you don't hear every day," Chester said. He pushed a button on a keychain he was holding and the car's alarm deactivated. Then he rushed to open the doors and helped everyone inside. When this was done, he hopped into the front seat and turned on the ignition.

"Buckle up," Chester said, slamming his foot on the gas. The car roared down the street after Cobweb.

Chester zipped around cars and pedestrians like a professional racecar driver. Sabrina quickly fastened her seat belt and then craned her neck out the window in hopes of spotting their quarry. She didn't have to search for long. Cobweb was directly in front of them, darting in and out of traffic.

Unfortunately, as Sabrina discovered when she peeked out the rear window, they were being followed, too. Tony Fats and Bobby Screwball were flying after them.

A blast of energy slammed into a nearby fire hydrant and Sabrina watched it explode, sending a geyser of water high into the air.

"They're shooting at us," Daphne said.

Chester made a quick left and then a right. He beat a couple lights but an unfortunate turn landed them right in bumper-to-bumper traffic. Cobweb soared over the cars ahead with ease. Meanwhile, Chester sat in the front seat, licking the back of his hands. Sabrina watched him. She'd almost forgotten he was a cat.

Daphne tapped Chester on the shoulder. "Can you open the sunroof?" she asked.

"*Liebling,* what are you thinking?" Granny Relda said.

"Don't worry, Granny," Daphne replied as she took the magic wand from her pocket. "I think I'm getting the hang of this."

When the sunroof slid open, Daphne stood up on the seat

so she was halfway out of the car and sent a flash of magic toward the traffic in front of them. Cars were jerked off to the side of the road as if by some invisible force. When the way was clear, Chester stomped on the gas pedal and they were off once more.

"You're going to get hurt," Sabrina said as she pulled Daphne back into the car.

"You're not the boss of me," Daphne snapped.

They raced into Times Square and came to a screeching halt when a crowd of pedestrians stepped out into the intersection. Cobweb soared over the tourists' heads, yet no one noticed. They were all too distracted by the dizzying lights and sights of Broadway. The dark fairy zipped down into a subway station and disappeared.

"Sorry, folks, I can't take the car down there," Chester said.

The group climbed out of the car just as Tony Fats and Bobby appeared. Hamstead had to leap out of the way of an incoming blast, which hit a stop sign instead and transformed it into a monkey. The monkey shrieked and disappeared into the crowd.

Daphne turned on the goons and fired a return volley. It hit the fairy godfathers dead on, and in a flash their feet were encased in concrete. With their wings unable to keep the extra weight aloft, the men crashed to the ground. Their wands tumbled out of their hands and rolled into an open sewer.

A crowd gathered around the family, stunned by what they had seen. Granny smiled nervously and reached into her handbag. Moments later the crowd had forgotten everything. When the people dispersed, Granny quickly took the magic wand from Daphne and handed it to Chester. "Would you be a dear and give this back to Twilarose?"

Chester nodded. "Sure, can I keep the car?"

"What are we waiting for? Cobweb is getting away!" Moth cried and raced away, down into the subway. The others hurried to follow.

As Sabrina helped Granny Relda down the steps to the subway below, she caught glimpses of Cobweb in the busy station. He'd hidden his wings and was trying to blend in with everyone else. When they reached the bottom of the steps, she saw him remove something from his pocket and swipe it at the subway turnstile. Then he stepped through and hurried to the platform just as a train pulled into the station.

Sabrina and Granny rushed to the turnstile, but without fare cards they were denied entry. Granny called out to Cobweb and the fairy turned to face her.

"If you're innocent then you will have a chance to prove it when you go to trial," Granny said.

"You fools, there is no justice in Faerie. There are no courts, no defenders. I would be tried and convicted by Titania herself. My head would be in the Hudson River by sunup."

The subway car doors opened and Cobweb stepped inside. Helpless, the family could only watch as the train disappeared into the tunnels.

"I will pursue him," Moth declared as her wings began to unfurl.

"No, you won't," Granny said, taking hold of Moth's arm.

"But he's getting away!" the fairy shouted.

"Yes, he is," the old woman said. "And we're letting him."

• • •

Granny ushered everyone into a nearby coffee shop and then asked one of its employees where the closest pay phone was located. The old woman bought everyone hot chocolate and then went outside in search of the phone.

"The old woman is a complete incompetent," Moth sneered. "We had Cobweb within our grasp and she let him go."

"You say another bad thing about my granny and you're going to get a sock in the nose," Daphne threatened.

Moth rolled her eyes.

Daphne turned to Mr. Hamstead. "What does *incompetent* mean?"

"She's saying that your grandmother isn't any good at her job," Hamstead replied.

Daphne shot the fairy girl another nasty look and then turned to her hot cocoa.

"So you don't need me with the big words, anymore?" Sabrina asked, trying not to sound too hurt.

"I never said I didn't need you, Sabrina. I just can't count on you," the little girl answered.

Granny returned, brushing snow off her coat. "All right, everyone, let's go," she said.

"Where are we going?" Daphne asked.

"To see Titania," the old woman said.

"What?" Sabrina cried. "She tried to kill us!"

Granny smiled. "I remember, *liebling.*"

• • •

Night had fallen by the time they reached Central Park. They found the Hans Christian Andersen statue, waited while a dark-haired woman walking a little West Highland White Terrier passed out of sight, then said the magic words. As before, the Golden Egg was revealed.

The damage to the restaurant from the night before had been cleaned up, and except for a few broken chairs in the corner, there was no sign that a disturbance had occurred at all. The place was empty except for a cat playing Irish jigs on a fiddle. Momma was behind the bar washing some glasses.

"Good to see you, folks," she said. "Care for something to eat? The kitchen's open."

"No, thank you," Granny said. "We're meeting Titania here."

The woman sighed. "And I just got this place cleaned up."

"Which Everafter are you?" Daphne asked.

The woman smiled. "Mother Goose, in the flesh, or in this case, in the feather." Suddenly, she transformed into a large black goose with a blue bonnet on its head. Daphne clapped and the goose changed back into the woman.

"So, you're part of the Grimm family," Momma said, as she turned back to her glasses. "I was so busy with customers I didn't get a chance to talk to you the other night. I knew Wilhelm pretty well. Nice guy. He was always trying to help. I guess it runs in the family. Veronica was the same way."

Sabrina sat down at a nearby table. "You knew my mother?"

Momma nodded. "Sweet lady. Helped me get into bartending school. Without her, I'd still be living at the Sunshine Hotel on the Bowery."

"The Sunshine Hotel?" Granny asked.

"Yeah, it's a flop house, one of those pay-by-the-day places. Real classy," Momma said sarcastically. "A few Everafters live there—the ones that can afford the rent."

"And the others?"

"They make do in shelters. Some of them live on the street."

"But you're magical beings," Sabrina said. "Why would you live so hard? You don't have to."

"Kiddo, just 'cause I can turn into a goose doesn't mean I don't have bills to pay. It ain't easy being an Everafter. None of us have identification. We can't get driver's licenses 'cause eventually people are going to notice that we aren't getting older. Getting a lease on an apartment without any credit history is impossible. Why, you can't even get a job without a social security number. Technically none of us exist. That's why Veronica was so well liked. She helped us find ways to work around the humans' rules. She cut the red tape when it was possible. When she disappeared, things went from bad to worse. Sad, too, as she told me she was working on a plan for us to help ourselves. She was supposed to give some big speech about it but then she disappeared."

Just then, Titania and Mustardseed appeared. Mustardseed stood close to his mother, holding her hand. Titania's heartbreak was plain on her face. She said hello to everyone, then turned her attention to Moth. "How is my son?"

Moth stepped forward with the cocoon. Titania took it in her hands and held it close to her face. "Get well, my son. You are needed." She handed the cocoon back to the small fairy and said, "Keep him safe."

"Oz said you needed to speak to us," Mustardseed prompted. He was so serious and mature. Sabrina studied his face, looking for signs that he was truly Puck's brother. They shared the same mouth and nose—that was about it.

"Yes, and this is difficult to say, but we can no longer help you solve Oberon's murder," Granny Relda said.

"What?" Daphne cried. Even Sabrina was surprised by her grandmother's words.

"Why?" Titania demanded.

"We were told that Cobweb killed your husband," Granny said. "But Cobweb claims he is innocent."

"Cobweb is lying!" Titania said.

"Maybe so," the old woman replied. "But he also says he cannot turn himself in because he would be executed immediately."

Mustardseed lowered his eyes.

"So it's true," Granny said.

"Of course it's true!" Titania screamed. "Murderers reap what they sow. That is the way of Faerie."

"So he will not be given a trial?" Granny Relda said.

Titania raged. "You are just like Veronica! She was always forcing her beliefs about justice on the rest of us. Cobweb killed my husband and I will oversee his execution myself!"

"Then you can find him without our help," Granny said.

"Veronica and I obviously share the same sense of right and wrong."

"I have never heard such treachery," Moth cried. "Who are you to tell us how to behave?"

"We will give him a trial," Mustardseed said quietly.

"You are overstepping your authority!" Titania raged at her son. "I am still Queen of Faerie."

"There is no Faerie, Mother. It has been gone for ten years," Mustardseed said. "We're living here, now. It's time to embrace our new home."

"You would throw away thousands of years of our history?" Titania argued.

"No, there is room for tradition," Mustardseed said. "But not traditions that oppress and create mistrust. Sentencing a man to die because that has always been the way of things is wrong. My father struggled for too long trying to rebuild that way of life. I will not allow you or anyone else to do the same. You will fail as he did."

"Mustardseed!"

"Mother, the humans have traditions of their own. Adopting a few of them might do us all a world of good. We will allow Cobweb to defend himself," Mustardseed said, and then turned to Granny Relda. "You have my word."

"Do we have hers?" Mr. Hamstead said, pointing at Titania.

Titania got up and stormed out of the room.

"I will make her understand," Mustardseed said.

Granny regarded the young fairy for a moment and then nodded. "And we will do our best to find Cobweb."

Mustardseed returned the nod, then turned and exited the room.

"So, I guess we're back to the subway," Daphne said.

"It's a place to start," said Granny. "Someone may have seen where he went."

"Or he may still be down there," said Momma. "It's a good place to hide from other fairies since they're technically forbidden to be in the tunnels."

"Great," Sabrina said. "Anyone got a flashlight and two years? Do you know how many miles of subway track there are? Six hundred and fifty six!" She recalled the report she had done in the fourth grade after a trip to the Transit Museum.

"It's the realm of the six dwarfs," Momma said. "They control the underground. If he's down there they'll help you find him."

Granny smiled. "And where would we find these dwarfs?"

• • •

Everyone agreed to continue the search for Cobweb in the morning. The sun had set long ago and it had grown bitterly cold, plus they were exhausted.

The group returned to the hotel to find Mr. Hamstead's room had been destroyed. His bed had been torn apart and his drawers rifled through. There was a note on the bathroom door that read, "You can go back to Ferryport Landing dead or alive. Your choice." Hamstead snatched the note and crumbled it into a ball.

"At least he gave me a choice," he said with a forced smile.

"Maybe I'm too much trouble for you," Bess said.

Hamstead shook his head. "I've dealt with bigger threats than Tony Fats."

Bess gave him a big hug and a kiss on the cheek. "You take care, doll face. I'll see you bright and early in the morning."

"I hope we get invited to the wedding," Daphne sang after the blonde beauty was gone.

Mr. Hamstead rolled his eyes but grinned from ear to ear. "I'm going to have the hotel put me in another room. You folks go get some rest. We've got a big day tomorrow."

Granny led Sabrina, Moth, and Daphne back to their room. Moth propped Puck's cocoon on the bed next to her and crawled under the covers. Sabrina lay next to her grandmother and sister in the other bed. She fell asleep listening to her sister plan Bess and Mr. Hamstead's wedding. That night, Sabrina dreamed of doves flying out of the top of a wedding cake.

• • •

When Sabrina woke the next morning, she crawled out of bed and went into the bathroom in hopes of finding a glass of water to get rid of her morning breath. She quietly shut the door so that her family and Moth could sleep. She gargled, washed her face, and checked herself in the mirror. Then she screamed.

Hovering several feet off the ground behind her was Puck's cocoon. She turned to find that the top of it had split open and something was gurgling inside. When she craned her neck to get a better look, a thick, green gas seeped out. It had the foulest smell Sabrina had ever experienced—like rotten cabbage, dirty laundry, and string cheese. Sabrina instinctively leaped back but the cocoon followed her, like a smelly puppy.

"Get this thing away from me!" Sabrina cried, but no one came. She tried to maneuver around it, but every step she took the cocoon mimicked. She faked to the left and then to the right, only to have the cocoon block the bathroom door, trapping her inside. Then the real nightmare started.

A sound like a steam whistle filled Sabrina's ears and green gas blasted out of the top of the cocoon, filling the bathroom with a funky fog. It seeped into Sabrina. It was in her hair, in her socks—she could even taste it. She pinched her nose tightly but it didn't help.

"Sabrina, are you okay in there?" her grandmother said as she tapped on the door.

"No!" Sabrina cried.

"It sounds as if your dinner isn't agreeing with you. Is there anything I can do? The hotel might have some antacids for your belly," the old woman said.

There was another knock on the door. "Hey! Light a match in there," Daphne shouted.

Suddenly, the door burst open and Moth shrieked in rage.

"*How dare you!*" she cried.

"My goodness gracious," Granny Relda said. "What is going on in here?"

"This thing just blew up on me," Sabrina cried as the cocoon continued to spray her with fumes. "Make it stop!"

"What you've done is unforgivable!" Moth seethed. "You have stolen my right!"

"I didn't steal anything!" Sabrina cried. "It followed me in here."

"Moth, could you tell us what is happening?" Granny asked.

Moth growled. "During the larval stage, when a fairy is most vulnerable, he chooses the one person in the world he trusts the most to look after him. Once the choice is made the cocoon marks the person with a special scent, one the cocoon can easily follow. This is an honor that should have gone to me."

"Well, then," Granny said as the last of the gas fizzed out of the top of the cocoon. "I suppose congratulations are in order."

The smell was all over Sabrina and no amount of washing could get it off. She took six showers, washed her hair, and scrubbed every inch of her body, but each time the smell returned with a vengeance. She could even smell it on her toothbrush. If she hadn't been so angry she might have cried.

Still, the smell was only half the nightmare. Sabrina discovered that wherever she went the cocoon hovered behind her, step for step. She shouted at it, hid from it, even threatened to drop-kick it out the hotel window, but nothing would stop it. As she couldn't reasonably walk the streets with a flying, eggplant-shaped gas bomb hovering at her shoulder, Granny and Daphne went out in search of something that might work as camouflage.

Left alone with an angry Moth, Sabrina ignored the fairy, watching talk shows she was certain were inappropriate for her. Moth stalked around the room with clenched fists, muttering bitter words under her breath.

"What's this?" Sabrina said when her grandmother and sister returned with a long piece of string.

Granny tied one end of the string to the bottom of the cocoon and handed the other end to Sabrina. "Now, isn't that a lovely balloon?"

Sabrina grumbled, knowing she looked like an unhappy child at the worst birthday party ever.

• • •

Mother Goose's directions were far better than any Bess or Oz had given the group. Momma knew exactly where to find the dwarfs. They lived in an abandoned subway station underneath the mayor's office downtown. The City Hall station had been closed decades ago, when the new, longer subway cars had made the platform impractical.

The walk to the station was chilly and the Grimms were glad to have scarves and mittens. Even Mr. Canis had found a big pair of gloves for his claws and a scarf to wrap around his whiskered head. Moth, Mr. Hamstead, and Bess didn't seem bothered by the cold, Moth because of her fairy blood and Mr. Hamstead and Bess because they were too busy giggling and holding hands to notice the temperature.

The group crossed a small park and found the steel door in the sidewalk that Momma told them led into the ancient subway station. There was no one out in the harsh weather, so they didn't have to worry about being seen when Canis pulled the door open, revealing a flight of steps that led down into darkness. Mr. Hamstead insisted that he go first, claiming his police training prepared him for any kind of danger. It was obvious his boasting was for Bess's benefit, but Sabrina held her tongue.

Hamstead led the group down the steps and when everyone was inside, Canis pulled the door closed, plunging them into darkness.

"Creepy," Daphne said.

"Just be patient, *liebling*. Your eyes will adjust," Granny promised.

"Man, it smells foul down here," Bess said.

"I believe that is the girl," Canis said.

"Uh, hello? I'm standing right here!" Sabrina said.

Before long, their eyes adjusted, and Mr. Hamstead was leading them along a damp concrete passageway lined with huge pipes and electrical wiring. Every once in a while they would pass under a dingy, flickering lightbulb, which helped them see a few feet ahead.

"We are close," Canis said, sniffing the air. "I smell them."

The tunnel opened into a huge station with an arched ceiling held up by elegant columns and cut through with skylights that allowed rays of light to shine down on the gold-tiled walls and floor. The room looked like the lost tomb of a pharaoh. At the center was a single train track, where a lone subway car was parked. Sabrina had been in many subway stations in New York City, but this one, by far, was the most beautiful.

"Hello?" Granny shouted out. Her voice bounced off the walls and echoed back. "Is anyone here?"

"They have obviously abandoned this station," Moth said.

Something flickered in the corner of Sabrina's vision. She spun quickly and thought she saw movement in the shadows along the far wall. She turned to Mr. Canis, whose senses were much more acute than hers. He held his finger to his lips to let her know he had seen something, too, and to be quiet.

"What are we waiting for?" Moth continued as she headed for the train car. "We should take their train and search the tunnels ourselves."

Before she could step into the car, the station erupted with movement as five tiny men bore down on them, flipping and jumping, shouting and screaming. They stopped just short of the group, surrounding them like tiny ninjas from a martial arts film.

The door to the subway car opened and a sixth little man with a long, white beard stepped out and eyed the group angrily through round glasses. He wore a blue uniform jacket with a patch that said MTA. Sabrina knew what the letters stood for—

Metropolitan Transit Authority. The little man worked for the subway.

"You're trespassing in the domain of the six dwarfs," he said, signaling to the others to close in on the group. "Invaders get a beating."

Sabrina watched as one of the little men slipped a set of brass knuckles on his hand.

Granny stepped forward. "We're not here to invade your territory."

A second dwarf clenched his fists. He had greasy little half spectacles on his nose. "These are our tunnels," he said. "We'll fight every one of you, chickadee!"

Mr. Canis growled. Sabrina could see he was losing his patience, again.

"We're looking for someone and we were told you could help," Sabrina said quickly. "A fairy flew down here last night. We think he's hiding in the tunnels."

"A fairy!" cried the dwarfs in horror. "No fairies in the subway! Your kind isn't welcome here."

"We're not fairies," Daphne said. "Well, except for her," she added, pointing at Moth. "We're detectives."

Suddenly, the white-bearded leader of the group cried out. "My oh my, it's you! It's Veronica's girls."

The little men immediately lowered their fists and smiled. They crowded around Sabrina and Daphne, offering up praise for their mother.

"Veronica was a gem."

"A real inspiration!"

"We loved her."

"What charisma!"

The men smiled and introduced themselves. Each had a different story about Sabrina and Daphne's mother. They all seemed to idolize her and regretted the day she had disappeared. The day of the "big speech," they added. It was clear they thought the speech would have changed their lives.

When it grew quiet again, the leader, who called himself Mr. One, spoke. "What are you doing down here?" he asked.

"We're looking for Cobweb," Daphne replied.

"Just like your mother," Mr. One said with a chuckle. "Veronica was always taking on other people's troubles. She wanted to help, even when it put her in some sticky situations. Your mother introduced me to my wife. Anything we can do to help you would be an honor."

"Can you help us search for Cobweb? We think he went underground in these tunnels," Hamstead said.

"Nobody knows these tunnels better than you do," Bess

added, and the dwarfs puffed up with pride at her compliment.

"What do you say, boys?" Mr. One asked his companions. "Up for a fairy hunt?" He pronounced the word *fairy* as one might the word *rat*. It was clear that dwarfs and fairies weren't fond of each other.

"Can we keep the train windows open?" Mr. Two asked, pointing his thumb at Sabrina. "Someone's a little funky."

Sabrina scowled.

Nevertheless, the other dwarfs cheered and raced for their subway car. The girls and their group followed. As they climbed aboard, Mr. One opened the conductor's door at the front of the car and stepped inside the control room. The rest of the dwarfs hurried to different parts of the train car. Mr. Two and Mr. Six made sure everyone got into a comfortable seat while Mr. Five and Mr. Three opened a couple panels on the wall. Inside each panel was a bright yellow handle. The dwarfs each pulled one down and suddenly there was a loud hiss and the train doors closed. Mr. One's voice came over the loudspeaker. "All passengers, welcome to the D train. Please, no eating, drinking, or playing loud music while onboard. Next stop . . . well, I guess we're just going to have to see. All right, everyone. Hold onto something! We're going express."

The train car suddenly surged forward, sending the little men tumbling and skidding across the floor. Sabrina and Daphne helped them to their feet, then grabbed onto the pole in the center of the car to steady themselves. They looked out the windows and saw they were rocketing through the tunnels.

"You wouldn't happen to know a Mr. Seven would you?" Daphne asked Mr. Two.

"He's my brother," the dwarf said.

"We know him. He lives in Ferryport Landing," Sabrina said.

Mr. Two frowned. "Well, next time you see him, remind him he owes me twenty bucks."

"What's with the balloon?" Mr. Five asked Sabrina as he lifted his little blue toboggan hat out of his eyes.

"It is King Puck's medicinal vessel!" Moth said indignantly.

"Smells like the N train coming back from Coney Island," Mr. Four grumbled.

Mr. Six snatched a walkie-talkie off his belt and held it to his mouth. "Kenny, this is Mr. Six. I'm in train 499. Have there been any unusual sightings in the tunnels today?"

A voice on the other end grunted. "You mean like six little people driving a stolen subway car through the system?"

Mr. Six scowled and turned to the group. "Kenny's a human.

We trust him—helped get him the job with the MTA—but he's a pain in the morning."

"Especially when he hasn't had his coffee," Mr. Four added.

"Kenny, I'm talking about fairies," Mr. Six said into the device. "You know, anyone report seeing a flying person with wings?"

There was silence on the other end and then Kenny responded. "Actually, there's a report of an incident at the Fifty-ninth Street station. Some woman claimed she saw an angel in the tunnel."

"Sounds like our fairy. When did it happen?" Bess asked.

Mr. Six repeated the question into his walkie-talkie.

"Five minutes ago," Kenny said.

"All right, pal, I'm on the 6 line coming up on Spring Street. I need to jump to the F line at Broadway-Lafayette."

"Thanks for the warning," Kenny said grumpily.

"Kenny, just do it!" Mr. Six shouted into the walkie-talkie. In no time, the train was racing into the Broadway-Lafayette station, where it jumped onto an intersecting track, forcing the car to make a hairpin turn. Nearly everyone fell out of their seat and onto the floor.

"Cobweb is lucky you guys are going to catch him," Mr. Two said, as he helped everyone back into their seats. "If we caught him down here we'd teach him a lesson he wouldn't soon forget. The tunnels belong to us."

"Like anyone else would want them, half-breed," Moth sneered.

"You'll be singing a different tune when we strike it rich down here," Mr. Four said as he scratched his sideburns. "There's diamonds down here somewhere. I can smell 'em. All we have to do is find them."

Mr. Six raised his hand for quiet and held his walkie-talkie to his mouth. "Kenny, Six here again. I need you to divert us to the uptown A track at West Fourth Street."

The car was suddenly diverted again and whipped through the next tunnel so fast Sabrina was sure they would derail.

"I got him!" Mr. One shouted over the loud speaker.

Everyone raced to join him at the front of the car. There, flying directly in front of the train, was Cobweb. He turned back to look at them and Sabrina saw his face. It was angry and desperate. His wings began to beat even harder and he zipped ahead into the tunnel.

"He's getting away, fool!" Moth cried. "Can't you make this thing go faster?"

"You got it!" One shouted.

The train car zipped through the tunnels, taking turns at blistering speeds. It slammed through one station after another, blasting waiting passengers with wind that blew their newspapers and coffee cups out of their hands. All the time, Mr. Six barked orders to Kenny on his walkie-talkie that sent the train jumping onto different lines. More than once they nearly collided with another train. If the constant near crashes bothered the dwarfs, they didn't show it. In fact, they seemed bored by the whole experience.

Cobweb was almost impossible to catch. He could easily switch to a different tunnel, or backtrack the way he came before the train car had a chance to maneuver. Still, the dwarfs did a good job of keeping up.

Just as they seemed almost on top of the fairy, there was a loud thump on the roof of the car.

The dwarfs looked at one another with serious expressions.

"What?" Mr. Canis growled.

Mr. Four held his finger to his lips urging him to be quiet. After a few seconds, there was another loud thump.

Mr. Five looked to the roof. "Uh oh."

"What's uh oh?" Granny cried.

"Yahoos," Five replied.

"Yahoos? What's a Yahoo?" Daphne asked.

"Dirty lunatics that keep invading our tunnels. Gulliver should have never brought them over here!" Mr. Six complained.

"You mean Gulliver? The Gulliver from *Gulliver's Travels?*" Sabrina asked.

"The same. He felt sorry for the little heathens and tried to civilize them by bringing them to the United States. They took over the Bowery and were happy enough playing in punk rock bands and working in coffee shops—you know, being worthless slackers—but now the neighborhood is being taken over by boutiques and health food stores. So they're in search of new turf and have been eyeing the tunnels all year."

There was another loud thump and one of the glass windows shattered. A thick, hairy hand reached into the car from outside. Mr. Six swatted at it. "Dirty, stinking slackers. Go find another neighborhood. Haven't you ever heard of Brooklyn?"

Then the entire train started rocking back and forth. Loud hooting and hollering could be heard, followed by more of the frightening pounding on the train.

"They're trying to derail us!" Mr. One shouted from his conductor seat. "If they keep rocking this train we're going to jump right off the tracks and slam into the wall."

"That's bad, isn't it?" Daphne asked the little men. They all nodded.

"I've got an idea!" Mr. Two said. "But you're not going to like it. Let's slam on the brakes."

The rest of the men stared at him.

"You're right, we don't like it," Mr. Six said. "We'll just derail ourselves."

"That's the idea!" Mr. Two cried. "We whip the car into South Ferry Station and then slam on the brakes."

"South Ferry is the end of the line, you imbecile!" Mr. Five shouted. "If we can't stop we'll crash."

"Even if we *can* stop, the train will probably catch on fire," Mr. Three cried. "The brakes can't handle the strain."

Another window shattered in the back of the train car.

Mr. Two shrugged. "It doesn't look like we have much choice. We can slam into the wall and get mangled in twisted metal or save ourselves but possibly die a fiery death."

"You fools cannot be serious," Mr. Canis said, rising to his feet. "Stop the train now, and I will get out and take care of these little parasites."

"No can do, buddy," Mr. Six said. "We're in a tunnel and these tracks are electrified. If you stepped on one you'd be an instant French fry."

"Grab onto something, people," Mr. One said over the loud-speaker. "Sorry we don't have any seat belts." The dwarfs scurried over to seats and hugged them tightly. The girls and their friends looked at one another in disbelief.

Mr. Six shouted into his walkie-talkie. "Kenny, we need you to clear the platform at South Ferry."

There was a groan on the other end of the line. "When?"

"Two minutes," Mr. Six replied.

"Two minutes?"

"Just do it, Kenny!"

Daphne wrapped her arms around Granny Relda. Even in all the excitement, Sabrina felt stung that the little girl would turn to their grandmother instead of her sister, who had been there for her whole life! Now, it was like Sabrina didn't even exist.

"South Ferry is the last and final stop on this train!" Mr. One said over the loudspeaker. Then he raced out of the conductor's room, climbed up onto one of the seats, and reached for a red cord on the wall. A sign above it read EMERGENCY BRAKE.

Mr. Hamstead wrapped his arms around Bess and pulled her to the floor.

"You gonna save my life again, cowboy?" she said.

Hamstead nodded. "That's my job."

"I hope this hurts!" Mr. Six shouted to the Yahoos on the ceiling just as Mr. One pulled the brake cord.

7

A loud, metallic screech filled the air. Sabrina was jolted forward but managed to grab the center pole as she soared past. Still, the forward momentum of the car nearly pulled Sabrina's arms out of their sockets.

Just then, the darkness of the tunnels turned to light. Sabrina knew they had just entered South Ferry Station. She saw three Yahoos with thick arms and legs tumble off the front of the train. They fell in horrible, bone-crunching fashion. But as black smoke began to fill the car, Sabrina wondered if the Yahoos were the lucky ones. She could see flames and sparks outside as the car came to a hard, jerky stop. She heard feet racing up and down the car, and then the doors opened.

"Everyone off!" one of the dwarfs shouted. Sabrina couldn't

be sure which one it was through the smoke. "This thing is going to go up in flames."

Mr. Two and Mr. Five helped Sabrina to her feet and hurried her onto the station platform, where everyone else was gathered. Puck's cocoon floated out of the car behind Sabrina.

Moth grabbed the cocoon's string and whirled around to confront the group. "You lost Cobweb, you fools," she cried.

"Shut your trap, Princess," Mr. Three said. "You're not so big that I can't put you over my knee."

Sabrina had no time for their stupid argument. She hugged her sister. "Are you OK?" She didn't wait for an answer. Instead, she started examining the little girl's arms and legs for broken bones or cuts.

"I'm fine," Daphne said, irritated. She struggled out of Sabrina's embrace.

"Good!" Sabrina said as she pretended not to be hurt. She looked around at the others. "We're all safe now. Everything is going to be OK. We're out of danger." It seemed as if one of them was always getting hurt on these detective missions; it was amazing to see her friends and family unscathed.

"Dwarfs go too far!" a voice shouted. Sabrina turned. One of the Yahoos, who only moments ago had been crumpled on the floor, was now back on his feet. His friends had joined him.

"You don't want any of this, monkey-boy," Mr. Six said. "We might be small but we'll lay the smackdown on all of you."

The Yahoos had a high-pitched sadistic laugh just like the hyenas Sabrina had once seen on a Discovery Channel documentary.

"We take tunnels. Tunnels ours!" they cried.

Mr. One stepped forward. Much to Sabrina's amazement, he moved into a fighting stance identical to one she had often seen Daphne take. It was an attack position that Snow White had taught the little girl in her Bad Apples Self-Defense class. The little man gestured to the Yahoos. "Come get some."

Then he and the five other dwarfs bowed to their opponents, as if they were in a martial arts movie. Daphne ran to join them before Sabrina could stop her.

"Present your warrior faces!" Mr. One shouted.

The six dwarfs and Daphne crinkled up their faces, roared like lions, and launched into an attack. The Yahoos were twice as big and, Sabrina guessed, ten times as strong, but the dwarfs were fast and nimble. They leaped and flipped like kung fu masters, avoiding blows and delivering painful kicks to their opponents' faces. Daphne was in the midst of the fight, punching and kicking, though far less gracefully than the little men. Sabrina had to stop her. This was why Daphne had to quit the family business. Someone always got hurt, and Sabrina wasn't going to let it be her sister. But before she could act, she felt a tap on her shoulder. Sabrina spun around and found Cobweb hovering over her.

"Was anyone injured?" he asked.

"It's over," Sabrina stammered, preparing to defend herself. "Mustardseed has promised you a fair trial. Turn yourself in."

"I did not kill Oberon," Cobweb said.

"Stop lying. Oberon said you did it. If you don't come with us now, we're going to catch you and your Scarlet Hand buddies, too.

"My what?"

"Don't play dumb with me. We know you're involved with them. You left their mark on Oberon's body."

"Child, I have no idea what you are talking about," Cobweb said. "I'm not in any group and I didn't kill Oberon!"

Moth spotted the dark fairy. "Murderer!" she cried. She reached into her pocket and took out a small flute, similar to the one Sabrina had seen Puck use many times. It summoned a tiny flying army of pixies he called his minions. Moth blew a few light notes and then shoved it back into her pocket.

Suddenly, a wave of little lights hit Cobweb in the chest. They surrounded him and collectively slammed him into a nearby wall. Sabrina could hear the wind fly out of his lungs.

Granny grabbed the fairy girl by the arm and shook her. "What are you doing, Moth?" the old woman cried. "Make them stop!"

Moth refused and pulled away.

But Cobweb fought off the little army and ran up the station stairs with the pixies in pursuit. Moth screamed and raced after them.

"We have to stop her," Granny said to the group.

"Wait. Daphne!" Sabrina cried. She'd lost track of her sister in the confusion. She spotted her celebrating with the dwarfs. Together they had successfully beaten the Yahoos back into the tunnels.

Sabrina raced over to her sister, clamped her hand around Daphne's arm, and dragged her up the station steps, with Granny and their friends following behind. Daphne shouted, "Hey, let go of me!" But Sabrina ignored her. So the little girl gave up and waved good-bye to the dwarfs instead, who were still celebrating their victory over the Yahoos. "Bye. Thanks!" Daphne called. "I'll tell Mr. Seven you said hello!"

"Tell him I want my twenty bucks!" Mr. Two cried.

"Good luck, daughters of Veronica!" the little men shouted.

When the girls reached the surface, Cobweb was gone. Moth paced nearby, screaming in rage. "We've lost him, again!"

"I don't know who you're screaming at," Mr. Hamstead said

angrily. "That psychotic little display of yours was why he escaped."

"You blame me?" Moth shouted. "How dare you talk to me in such a manner."

"*Child!*" Mr. Canis roared. "You have tested my patience long enough today!" He leaped forward, talons already drawn as if prepared to rip the fairy to shreds.

"Wolf!" Hamstead shouted, stepping in between Moth and the old man. "Back away."

Canis eyed Hamstead for several moments.

"I can see you in there, mongrel," Hamstead said. "You come out and you'll get more of what the Three Little Pigs gave you before."

Something inside of Canis seethed but it did what it was told. Most of the old man's wolflike features shrank away.

Hamstead turned and addressed everyone. "We need to regroup here, folks. We're trying to catch Cobweb. Not kill him." He looked at Moth. "And we shouldn't be fighting among ourselves. If anyone can't work as a team, *she* should go back to the hotel. 'Cause to be honest, you're in the way. But if you want to catch our suspect, and he is only a suspect right now, then let's start working together."

Bess gave Hamstead an admiring look and a squeeze on the

arm. Moth, however, gave the portly ex-policeman an angry scowl and muttered something offensive under her breath.

"Look, he left footprints in the snow," Daphne said, finally pulling free of her sister.

"Daphne Grimm! Well done!" Mr. Hamstead said. "If we follow these prints they'll lead us right to him."

Everyone nodded, even Moth, and they set out to follow the tracks.

As they walked, Sabrina tried to engage her sister.

"That was stupid of you to get into that fight," she said.

"You're stupid," Daphne said.

"You could have been hurt. Why would you take such a risk?"

"I'm going to have to take bigger risks now that I'm on my own," Daphne replied.

Sabrina stopped in her tracks, and watched as her sister hurried to catch up with Mr. Canis, who was leading their group.

Granny joined Sabrina and gave her a sad smile. "This is her choice, *liebling*."

"So I should just let her get killed?"

Granny shook her head. "As long as I'm around I won't let that happen."

The prints led into Battery Park. In warmer weather, the park would be filled with tourists waiting for the boats to the Statue of Liberty and Ellis Island. Now it was almost empty. The Staten Island Ferry, a commuter boat that took people to the city's remote island borough, docked nearby as well, and it was into the ferry terminal that Cobweb's tracks led. Sabrina helped her grandmother up the snow-covered ramp to the waiting room inside. There the group drew many stares from the terminal staff. Sabrina realized that most were gazing at Mr. Canis—all seven feet of him.

"Look, there's Cobweb!" Moth shouted. Sabrina turned in the direction the fairy girl pointed only to see a boat pulling away from the dock. Cobweb sat on the railing looking back at them. His face was grim and cold.

"I'll get him!" Moth said as her fairy wings popped out of her back.

Granny snatched her arm and held the girl back. "We'll wait for the next boat."

Moth reluctantly retracted her wings.

"By the time we get to Staten Island, Cobweb will be long gone," Daphne said.

"You have bigger problems than that," a rough voice said from behind them. Sabrina turned around and saw a half-dozen men with skin the color of copper and jet-black hair coming toward them. Their leader had dark eyes as fierce as any she had ever seen. He spoke again, "You know as well as I do that fairies are not welcome on docks controlled by Sinbad the Sailor."

Sabrina instinctively stepped between her sister and the stranger. She'd read *The Arabian Nights* recently, researching jinnis that might help her rescue her parents. The story of Sinbad was fresh in her memory. He'd gone on seven voyages and each trip had nearly killed him, though he had seen some fairly amazing things, including ogres, jinnis, and fish disguised as massive islands. He'd killed hordes of monsters, too. She didn't remember him as a villain, but she'd learned the hard way that sometimes the good guys switched sides.

"Is that so?" Moth said angrily to Sinbad. "Well, what are you going to do about it?"

The sailor's men pulled nasty-looking daggers out of their coats.

"No fairies on the ferry," Sinbad said. "Oberon may have been able to force us to pay his lousy taxes, but he's dead. I'm not about to let some other fairy come in and take our hard-earned money."

"We're not fairies," Daphne said. "We're detectives and we're trying to find the person who killed Oberon."

Sinbad cocked an eyebrow. "Praise be! Can it be you? Can it be that I am in the presence of Veronica Grimm's children?"

Daphne nodded, and the men put their daggers away.

"I am honored to meet you," Sinbad said. "It was a dark day in my heart when your mother vanished. What brings you here?"

"The fairy who killed King Oberon is on the boat that just left," Granny Relda said.

Sinbad looked at his men and then looked back at the group. "I may be of some assistance," he said and led everyone to the next docking station. He took out a key, unlocked a huge door, and slid it open. Behind it was a second ferryboat.

"You've got your own boat?" Hamstead asked.

"I *am* the harbormaster for the Staten Island Ferry," Sinbad said proudly. He helped them onboard, then led them up a flight of steps to the bridge. He started the boat's engine as his men untied its mooring lines from the dock. When the boat was free, the men shouted up to their captain, and he pulled down a lever, easing the ferry away from the dock with expert care. In no time they were cruising away from Manhattan in pursuit of Cobweb.

"Chasing a murder . . . is this not dangerous work for young girls?" Sinbad asked.

"We're Grimms, this is what we do," Daphne said.

Sinbad laughed. "Your mother used to say the same thing whenever I had to help her out of one of her many close calls. Not that I minded. I have to admit, I myself was much smitten with her."

"You had a crush on our mother?" Daphne asked.

"I'd hardly call it a crush. I was head over heals, to be honest. Veronica was quite a woman and I've known a great many in my day. She was brilliant and strong, if a bit stubborn."

"Sounds like someone I know," Granny said, flashing Sabrina a smile.

"I asked her to run away with me nearly a thousand times, but she always rebuffed me. She said she had eyes for only one man. I suppose it was your father she spoke of. The fates were smiling on him the day he met her."

Sabrina was livid. Hearing him talk about her mother this way was infuriating. Sinbad noticed and smiled.

"Little one, allow a man to dream. Your mother never took my advances seriously. Most of the time she was too busy with her big plan to fix our community to even notice I was flirting."

One of Sinbad's crew raced to the bridge. He looked nervous and sweaty. "My lord, we have a big problem."

"What is it?"

"Pirates!"

"Again!" Sinbad scowled. "It is the third time this week!"

"Pirates? What pirates?" Sabrina cried, but Sinbad rushed out onto the deck with his man. The Grimms and their friends dashed after him and found the entire crew standing on one side of the boat peering at something through binoculars.

Sabrina snatched a pair of binoculars from the nearest sailor and scanned the horizon. Sailing near the Statue of Liberty was a boat with a black flag waving in the wind. The flag had a skull and crossbones on it.

"You've got to be kidding me," Sabrina said, handing the binoculars to her grandmother.

Just then, an enormous explosion could be heard coming from the pirate boat. A moment later something big crashed into the water not far from the ferry.

"They dare fire on me? Sinbad? Master of the sea? Turn this ship toward them and see how brave they are with our cutlasses at their throats," the captain cried. His men cheered and several raced to the helm. The ferry made an abrupt turn and headed straight for the approaching pirates.

"Turn this ship around!" Mr. Canis cried. "We're after a killer. We have no interest in your petty turf war!"

"You have nothing to fear, my large friend, praise be. I am Sinbad and I have faced these foul vermin before. Of course, maybe we should arm you. Men, hand out some steel!"

The men shoved large swords into everyone's hands.

"What are we supposed to do with these?" Sabrina asked, alarmed.

"They're quite useful for killing pirates," Sinbad said as he hurried back to the bridge.

"I don't think I'm allowed to kill pirates!" Daphne called after him. She looked up at Granny Relda. "Am I?"

The old woman shook her head, collected the children's swords, and handed them to one of Sinbad's men.

Another of the crew rushed toward them with life jackets.

"What do we need these for?" Hamstead asked as there was another loud splash off the side of the boat.

"In case we have to jump," the man replied.

"Why would we have to jump?"

"If the boat were about to blow up," the sailor said as if he were talking about something as ordinary as gardening or making toast.

Hamstead cringed and turned to Sabrina. "Pigs don't swim," he whispered nervously.

There was an enormous crash, and the cabin wall they were standing next to exploded, sending wood and glass everywhere. Sabrina tumbled to the floor.

"We've taken a hit!" Sinbad shouted. "It's time to show those devils what kind of men we are! Let's do this old school, shall we?"

The crew roared in approval. One of Sinbad's men rushed to a panel on the wall. Inside was a red button, which he pounded hard with his fist. He turned to the passengers with a wide smile. There was an odd mechanical grinding and then the sound of rockets firing. Suddenly, the top of the ferry flew off and crashed into the water. A hole opened up in the deck and a long wooden pole soared skyward. Farther down the deck, an identical pole was rising, and when both had extended as far as they could, huge rolls of fabric unfurled from the top. The fabric squares had ropes attached to their corners. It quickly dawned on Sabrina that they were sails, and the crew went about tying them into position. The cold winter wind heaved against the boat and Sabrina felt it pick up speed.

Sinbad's voice rose above the noise, saying, "Stand clear for artillery upload."

Suddenly more slots opened along both sides of the boat and out poked heavy black cannons, each with a pyramid of cannonballs stacked next to it. Several of the men rolled huge wooden kegs into place next to the cannons. The kegs had the words GUNPOWDER and DANGER printed on the side.

"We have to get off this thing!" Sabrina cried. She grabbed her sister and grandmother and raced to the edge of the boat, looking back to make sure Puck's cocoon and the rest of her group were safely behind her. Then she turned and peered into the black water below and realized how very cold it would be—the freezing temperature would mean almost certain death. They were trapped onboard, and worse, the crew of the ferry seemed to be loving the situation. When a cannonball landed just short of the boat and splashed into the water, they booed as if they were disappointed in their attackers' aim.

"Ladies, would you like to set off the return volley?" Sinbad asked, suddenly appearing before them, sword gleaming at his side. He was holding a flaming torch, which he offered to them.

Sabrina looked at the weird smile on the man's face. He was enjoying this nightmare. He might have been good to her mother, but it seemed he couldn't care less if Veronica's family were blown to bits. Sabrina thought about how she so often found herself in these situations, the kind where people got hurt, and she wasn't going to take it anymore. Without even thinking it through, she lunged forward, snatched the sword from Sinbad's belt, and leveled it at his head.

"Take us back to the dock," she said calmly.

"You look so much like your mother right now," Sinbad said, shifting his eyes back and forth from her face to the sword pointed at his throat.

"I've had enough of this craziness. Turn the boat around and take us back to the dock. You're not going to get us killed, especially before I get to retire," she said.

"Child, we are in the middle of a fight. If we turn this boat, the pirates will fire on our port side and we'll surely go down," Sinbad explained.

"Sabrina, give him back the sword," Granny Relda demanded.

"NO! This is exactly what I'm talking about when I say I don't want to be a Grimm. Look at these maniacs. They're having fun. And you know why? Because they can't die unless someone tries really hard to kill them. This is just a stupid game to them. Well, I can die, Granny, and so can you and Daphne. So, Sinbad here is going to turn this boat around right now."

Daphne rushed to Sabrina's side and snatched the sword away. "You're being a jerkazoid!" she shouted.

"I'm trying to protect us. I'm trying to save us all!" Sabrina cried.

"So is he," Daphne said, pointing at Sinbad. "Those pirates fired on us first."

She handed Sinbad back his weapon.

"You're a spirited girl," Sinbad said to Sabrina. "If a bit odd-smelling."

Before Sabrina could argue with her sister, she heard a hollow horn blast and watched as the men adjusted the sail riggings and tied them down tight. The sails trapped the wind, and again the ferry raced across the water. Sabrina could hardly believe the power of the blustery winter air; the boat was cutting through the waves as if propelled by rockets.

Sinbad took out his binoculars again and peered through the lenses. "We're close enough to see the faces of the mongrels now." He handed the binoculars to Hamstead, who took a peek as well.

"Uh, those aren't pirates," Hamstead said. "They're wearing suits and ties."

Sabrina snatched the binoculars out of his hand and saw that Hamstead was right. The approaching boat wasn't a pirate ship at all but a yacht. Its passengers were wearing black tuxedos and seemed to be sipping cocktails between cannon shots.

"Is this a joke?" Sabrina said, yanking on Sinbad's sleeve.

"What do you mean?" the roguish sailor said.

"Those aren't pirates. They look like they work on Wall Street."

"What's the difference?" Bess asked.

Just then, the bridge above exploded. A cannonball had smacked into it, sending wood and glass in all directions. The two men steering the boat had jumped to safety at the last second.

Sinbad shouted to his men. "They're coming alongside! Let's show them what we're all about, praise be."

The men cheered, and when the "pirate" boat was close enough, Sinbad leapt onto it and started fighting a man wearing a three-piece suit who was brandishing a nasty-looking dagger. The two fought fiercely, their blades slashing through

the air. Several of the pirates, who were also very well dressed, mimicked Sinbad's bravery and jumped from the yacht onto the ferryboat. Sinbad's crew charged them, and a savage battle began. In no time, the family found themselves in the midst of clanging blades and shooting sparks.

Mr. Canis snatched up Sabrina and Daphne, and led Granny and Moth through the melee, doing his best to avoid getting slashed himself. Puck's cocoon floated close behind, missing several near punctures. Hamstead and Bess followed, and together they all raced down a flight of steps that led into the boat's hull. Unfortunately, they were followed by an ugly brute with a wicked scar running from the tip of his right eye to the edge of his lip. He was dressed as well as the other pirates but his clothing didn't lend him any charm. He roared at the family, and Canis roared back. The pirate stood there for a moment, apparently trying to understand who or what Canis was, and then ran back up the steps.

"The rest of you stay down here and hide. I should go and see if I can be of some help," Mr. Canis said.

"Me, too," Hamstead added.

"Ernest, be careful," Bess said, squeezing his pink hand.

In a flash, the two men were back up the steps and gone from view.

"You heard him, girls," Relda said. "Keep safe and keep moving."

They ran through the boat, looking for a safe nook to scurry into, but the boat was completely overrun by pirates. A wave of them stampeded down the steps and cornered the women.

"Hostages!" one of them exclaimed as he licked his blade.

The rest laughed.

"Take 'em to Silver," the first man shouted, and the pirates rushed at the women. Daphne kicked one in the shin and he fell to the floor in pain. Granny smacked another with her heavy handbag and split his lip open. Bess and Moth threw punches. Sabrina, on the other hand, was quickly grabbed around the neck, but she instinctively jammed her elbow into her attacker's belly. The rogue bent over as the wind flew out of him and he dropped his sword. Daphne snatched it off the floor and smacked him in the behind with the flat of the blade. It didn't do any permanent damage but from the groan the pirate uttered, it had obviously stung. Moth took a life preserver off the wall and brought it crashing down on the man's head. He fell to the floor unconscious.

Much to Sabrina's surprise, the pirates broke off their assault and backed away before rushing up the steps and disappearing.

"We make a pretty good team, don't we, ladies?" Bess crowed.

But they had only a minute to celebrate. The pirates returned with reinforcements. They managed to grab Sabrina, Daphne, and Moth, hauling the girls up onto the deck and then hoisting them over the side of the ship, where each landed unceremoniously on the deck of the yacht. Puck's cocoon, never far from Sabrina, floated after them. Seconds later all of the pirates were off the ferry and back on their own boat, which zipped across the river, leaving Sinbad, his crew, Granny Relda, Mr. Canis, Mr. Hamstead, and Bess far behind.

"The harbor belongs to Silver!" one of the pirates bellowed toward the ferry, causing all the rogues to cheer and raise their swords in the air. Many of them broke into song and danced little jigs. The girls didn't get to see much of this gloating. They were dragged roughly down a flight of steps toward the belly of the yacht.

"Get your hands off me, filth," Moth demanded. "I am a princess of the royal court."

"Listen, fairy," one of the pirates said in a thick English accent. "Get yourself through that door."

"And if I don't?" she said.

"Then you're going to miss the party," the other pirate said.

He opened the door and Sabrina gawked at what she saw inside. There were dozens of well-dressed men and women on a small dance floor in the center of the room. A disc jockey was spinning records and a glittery disco ball was flashing light around the room. Several of the dancers were gathered around a limbo pole near a banner that read HAPPY HOLIDAYS TO EVERY-ONE AT SILVER AND HAWKINS!

"What is this?" Sabrina asked.

"It's our firm's Christmas Party," the pirate replied.

"What?" the girls said in unison.

A tall gray-haired man hobbled over to them. He had a parrot on his shoulder and walked with a cane. He set down his drink and extended his hand to the captives, but none of them took it.

"So good of you to join us. I'm John Silver," he said.

Sabrina and the others said nothing.

"As in Long John Silver," he continued.

Still, the girls were silent.

"As in *Treasure Island,* documented by Robert Louis Stevenson," Silver said proudly.

"You're the bad guy then?" Daphne asked. "I've seen the movie about you. You're not very nice."

"Everyone has seen that lousy movie. Doesn't anyone read anymore?" the pirate asked with a scowl. "The book really captures more of my complexities."

The pirates roared with laughter.

"Aren't you supposed to have a peg leg?" the little girl asked.

Silver lifted his pant cuff to reveal a prosthetic leg. "This one here is the latest model."

"You'll regret this, pirate," Moth seethed.

The crowd booed.

"*Pirate* is such an ugly word," Silver explained. "Pirates are criminals. This is the twenty-first century. We've traded in doubloons and treasure for stocks and bonds."

The parrot squawked. "Buy low, sell high!"

"Then why did you attack us?" Sabrina asked.

"Money, little lady, money. Controlling the ports is a lucrative business, especially now that Oberon isn't around to stop us. The king extorted a lot of money from us. Now we've got an opportunity to get it back."

"So, you shot cannons at the Staten Island Ferry over turf? Aren't you worried that someone is going to notice?" Sabrina said.

"Kid, they may call New York the city that never sleeps but they should call it the city that never notices. We could sail up the East River and attack the mayor's mansion and I doubt it would even make the papers."

"Well, then, we don't want to get in the way of your little party. Why don't you drop us off at the dock and we'll let you get back to your fun," Sabrina said.

The crowd erupted into laughter.

"I'm afraid that's not possible," Silver said. "You see, you're not exactly guests, you're hostages."

"What does *hostages* mean?" Daphne asked.

"It means we're prisoners he's going to use to bargain with," Sabrina said.

"We're selling you to the highest bidder. The children of Veronica Grimm have to be worth something, not to mention a princess of the royal court to sweeten the pot. Friends, we're going to get one enormous holiday bonus!"

Everyone cheered.

"Now, rules of the sea are we treat our prisoners with civility, so help yourselves to the buffet. The DJ will be playing for another half hour and then we're going to do some karaoke. Relax, try to have some fun, but don't even think about singing 'Love Shack.' That's *my* song."

"Silver!" Moth cried. "When Titania finds out that you not only prevented the capture of a known murderer but also violently kidnapped me, you'll wish you were dead. You will never get away with this."

"I never get tired of hearing people say that to me," the pirate said, joining the others in a raucous laugh.

Moth snarled and then spit in the pirate's face. Silver calmly reached into his pocket and pulled out a handkerchief. He cleaned the spittle from his cheek, put his handkerchief back, then took a long curved knife from the cheese table and aimed the point at Moth's throat.

"You have a nasty mouth," Silver said. "Though I suppose I could fix that by cutting your tongue out."

The crowd roared its approval.

Suddenly, there was a bright flicker at one of the port windows. Sabrina looked out but didn't see anything. Maybe all the stress was getting to her.

"Leave her alone," Daphne pleaded. "She won't be any more trouble."

"Shut your yap, child!" Silver shouted as he dropped his cane and grabbed Daphne by the throat. "I'd hate to lose you, too, but I'm sure one Grimm girl would be just as valuable as two."

"Take your hands off her," Sabrina cried as she rushed at the rogue. He swung his knife away from Moth and toward her throat, stopping within the tiniest fraction of an inch of her skin.

"Keep it up, girlie, and you'll be able to breath out of your neck," he said.

Just then, the door into the hull flew off its hinges. A dark figure stepped down into the room. It was Cobweb.

"Run, girls!" he shouted, then opened his mouth and shot a

stream of fire at the pirates. They fled in every direction, giving Sabrina enough time to snatch her sister and Moth and rush them back up the steps onto the deck of the yacht. She peeked back and found Puck's cocoon following closely behind.

"Did he just save us?" Daphne said.

Sabrina shrugged. "Let's worry about getting off this boat. He might come back up here and change his mind."

The girls searched the ship but there was no lifeboat to be found; and worse, the pirates were already charging up onto the deck. Long John Silver hobbled up from below, followed by a dozen angry men with daggers. Two of them were dragging Cobweb along.

"You know, there's one thing I've learned during my time on Wall Street—you have to weigh the value of investments," Silver bellowed as he came toward the girls, who were now trapped against the ship's railing. "Take you Grimms, for instance. The both of you could be worth your weight in gold, but then again, it might be just as valuable to me to watch you and your fairy friends walk the plank."

"Dump the stock, now!" the pirate's parrot shrieked from his shoulder. "Sell! Sell! Sell!"

One of Silver's men rushed up from below with a long piece of wood and set it on the edge of the yacht. Once it was secure,

Silver pulled the cheese knife out of his belt and forced Sabrina to climb up on the plank.

"Don't hurt my sister!" Daphne yelled. She tried to grab at Sabrina's shirt to pull her back on deck, but one of the pirates yanked the little girl away.

"Let them go, Silver," Cobweb demanded. A pirate punched him in the belly to quiet him.

"Wait your turn," the man croaked.

Sabrina walked to the edge of the plank and looked down at the icy water. *This is the second time I've been on one of these things,* she remembered. Puck had forced her to walk a plank above their neighbor's pool the first time they met. He had used his pixies to get her up on the board. *Pixies.*

"Excuse me," Sabrina said. "Don't I get a last request?"

Silver smiled. "Indeed. Name it."

"I'd like my good friend Moth to play us a song on her flute. Something happy before we die."

"You are as dumb as a cow!" Moth cried. "You get one last wish and this is it?"

Sabrina looked at Daphne. "Yes, a song like the one Puck used to play for us. One so sad it stings."

Daphne's eyes grew wide with understanding. "Yes, Moth, play a song on your flute."

Cobweb cocked his eyebrows, showing Sabrina that he understood what she wanted. "Princess, might I suggest a particular song? I've always loved 'Flight of the Pixies.'"

Moth took her wooden flute out of the folds of her dress. Sabrina wasn't sure the little fairy understood what they wanted her to do, but she lifted the instrument to her mouth and blew a few short notes. When she was done, nothing happened.

"Uh, wasn't there a second verse?" Sabrina said. Maybe they were too far from shore for the pixies to hear them.

"No, there isn't a second verse," Moth snapped.

"Then play it again!" Sabrina cried.

Moth lifted the flute again and blew the same notes.

"All right, that's enough," Silver said.

"But wait, you filthy crab, what about your last request?" Moth asked.

"Why would I need a last request?" Silver said.

"Because you're about to be attacked," the little fairy girl replied. A split second later, the entire yacht was enveloped in an enormous swarm of dancing lights. They swirled around the pirates, who swatted at them with little effect. The pixies were everywhere, and they were stinging with all their might. Silver swung his dagger wildly as little dots of blood appeared on his face. The pirates raced into the belly of the boat, hoping to escape the swarm and letting go of Cobweb in an effort to protect themselves. When he realized his men were gone, Silver hobbled quickly after them.

The wave of pixies became one giant mass that hovered next to Moth, awaiting her orders. The little princess stepped over to Cobweb, who had fallen on the deck and was trying to catch his breath.

"And now I will deal with you," Moth said.

"I'm innocent," Cobweb begged. "I would never hurt Oberon. I supported his efforts to rebuild Faerie. He trusted me with the taxes. We were going to build a hospital, and a school for our children. I believed Faerie could be rebuilt. Why would I kill the only man who could accomplish all of it?"

"What are you talking about?" Sabrina cried.

"I was Oberon's counsel. The money we got from the citizens we were using to make everyone's lives better. We were preparing to announce the opening of a shelter for homeless Everafters. They were Oberon's ideas and I was working to make them reality."

Sabrina was stunned. She had despised Oberon from the moment she met him, even secretly felt that his death was justified, especially after hearing about his goons extorting money from the citizens and bullying everyone into obedience. But now, Cobweb was telling her that the king was a good man—or at least, was trying to be. It didn't make sense that Cobweb would kill a person he respected so much. Sabrina turned to her sister, who was just as amazed, and then to Moth. The little fairy was not moved by the story. In fact, she had murder in her eyes.

"Take him!" Moth shouted, and the pixies swarmed around the dark fairy. Cobweb staggered to his feet and his wings popped out of his back. Seconds later he was aloft. He was faster than the swarm and was out of their reach in seconds.

"Use the cannon," Moth instructed, and the swarm returned to hover around the big gun, using their collective mass to load a ball inside and then fill it with gunpowder.

"Moth, don't!" Daphne cried. "This isn't how we do things."

The fairy girl ignored her and stepped over to the cannon. She opened her mouth and a stream of fire shot out, igniting the cannon's wick. There was an earth-shaking roar and the deck buckled beneath them. Sabrina managed to right herself long enough to watch the black missile speed into the air and slam into Cobweb's back. The fairy fell from the sky and plunged into the waters.

"*No!*" Sabrina cried. She found a life preserver and tossed it overboard, knowing it was pointless. Even an Everafter couldn't survive that kind of injury.

In the distant waters, Sabrina spotted a flashing blue light heading in their direction. "This is the Coast Guard," a booming voice called out. "Lower your weapons and prepare to be boarded."

Moth turned to the girls. "Your job was to find Oberon's killer. He is dead. You are no longer needed. Find your grandmother and your friends and go back to the mud hole you call home."

She gestured for the pixies to swarm around Puck's cocoon. They latched onto it as Moth's wings sprang forth and she lifted into the air. She flew off, carefully guarding the cocoon as it fought and resisted being taken from Sabrina.

8

abrina and Daphne were taken into custody by social services. A friendly man named Mr. Glassman, who insisted they call him Peter, spent several hours trying to track down Granny Relda. By the time she arrived to claim the girls, it was nearly two in the morning and friendly "Peter" had lost his patience.

"These children were found on a yacht in the middle of the New York harbor, Mrs. Grimm," Peter said sternly. "The boat was filled with alcohol."

Granny smiled uncomfortably and shifted in her seat. "This has all been a misunderstanding. The girls and I got separated and—"

"So *you* were supposed to be on this yacht, too?"

"Why no—"

"We told you what happened. We were kidnapped," Daphne said.

"Young lady, the police have searched the boat. There was no one on it. In fact, the owner, a Mr. John Silver, is thinking of pressing charges against you for stealing it from the marina."

"Forgetful dust," Daphne grumbled. The pirates had used it to make a clean getaway.

Sabrina kicked her sister under the table and shook her head. The less crazy their story sounded the better off they would be.

The social worker took a deep breath. "Yes, the forgetful dust you keep telling me about. Children, I was your age once. I had imaginary friends, too. They're fun and they can even be healthy, but you need to learn the difference between reality and fantasy."

"Well, I think the girls learned their lesson," Granny said. "I'm sure you have other things to worry about. I'll take the girls and get out of your hair."

"Mrs. Grimm, you seem like a sweet lady but I'm afraid that's impossible," Peter said. "We need to evaluate your parenting skills. We can't just let you take the girls with you."

"How long will this evaluation take?" Granny asked.

"A few weeks at least."

A few weeks!" the girls cried.

Daphne nudged Granny. "Throw some forgetful dust on him."

Granny shook her head. "I'm all out."

Peter rolled his eyes. "In the meantime, the state will retain custody of the girls until we can determine if they *should* be returned to your care," he explained.

"But who's going to take care of them?" Granny Relda asked anxiously.

Just then, there was a knock on the office door. Standing on the threshold was a rail-thin woman with a face Sabrina knew and could never forget. She had thin lips, a hooked nose, and dull gray hair.

"Hello, Ms. Smirt," Peter said. "Please come in."

• • •

The orphanage was exactly as Sabrina remembered. Much like Ms. Smirt, it was nasty and drained of color. The floors were still filthy and the kids still miserable, and the moth-eaten sheets still smelled of mildew.

Smirt led them through the main sleeping room, which was little more than a hallway with two rows of tightly packed cots, filled with sleeping children. Sabrina and Daphne were assigned the last two empty beds and then forced to change into what Smirt called "orphanage attire," bright orange jumpsuits that reminded Sabrina of prisoners' clothes. When the girls were changed, Ms. Smirt led them to her office, where they were ordered to sit down.

Smirt eyed the girls with contempt. "Imagine what a surprise it is to see my favorite orphans, Sally and Denise."

"First, we're not orphans," Sabrina replied. "Second, I'm Sabrina and this is Daphne."

"Yes, the Grimm sisters, the bane of my existence," the woman replied.

"Listen, let's cut to the chase," Daphne said. "You're going to send us to live with some nutcase and we're going to escape like we always do. You should probably just send us back to live with our grandmother. At least then we are out of your hair."

Sabrina was stunned by her sister's bold speech. It sounded like something Sabrina herself might have said.

Smirt smiled, a frightening sight. "Well, if you would kindly explain your plan to the city, I'm all for it. Unfortunately, I'm required by law to keep trying to place you in a good home no matter how pointless it all seems."

The caseworker opened a drawer in her desk, took out some forms, and scribbled some notes. Sabrina could read them upside down. Smirt had written "incorrigible troublemakers" on the form and underlined it after adding several exclamation points at the end.

"I have some good news for you girls," the caseworker offered. "I've already found you a foster home that is willing to take you in."

"We don't want to go to a foster home. Our grandmother is going to take us back as soon as she can," Daphne said.

"I highly doubt that. The orphanage doesn't make a habit of letting people take care of children who encourage them to risk their lives on the high seas. Maybe someday . . . when I'm in charge," Smirt said wistfully. "But for now you're going to live with a Mr. Greeley."

Their caseworker snatched a folder off a stack of books and opened it. Sabrina noticed the title of the book on top. It was called *The Purpose-Driven Life*.

"Mr. David Greeley is currently in prison but he's getting out tomorrow and will pick you up as soon as he has met with his parole officer," Smirt said.

"Prison! What was he in prison for?" Sabrina said.

"Hmmm, let me see. Oh, here it is. Murder," the caseworker said.

"Murder?" the girls cried, nearly jumping out of their chairs.

"Yes, he murdered someone. No, I'm wrong. That was someone else," Ms. Smirt said.

Sabrina caught her breath and eased back in her seat.

"No, Mr. Greeley murdered several people. Seven to be exact. Beat them to death with a crowbar," Smirt said.

"You're going to send us to live with a serial killer?" Sabrina said.

"No, I'm sending you to live with a *former* serial killer. Mr. Greeley is rehabilitated. Now, off to bed with you. Newbies have to fix breakfast for everyone so you better get some sleep."

Smirt shoved the girls down the hall and back into the sleeping area. They found their beds among the rows of snoring, groaning children, and crawled underneath the scratchy blankets. Sabrina's cot was next to a window that had a baseball-sized hole in it. The cold wind blew directly onto her feet, so she tucked herself into a ball for warmth. Before Ms. Smirt left, she handcuffed the girls to their beds.

"Well, I suppose you're happy now," Daphne said when Smirt had scurried back to her office.

"Happy? Why would I be happy about this?"

"Isn't this what you wanted? To get away from Granny, the Everafters, and Ferryport Landing? Now you can pretend none of it ever happened."

"Daphne, I—"

"Every step you fought her. You've complained and disobeyed and been a real—"

"Jerkazoid?"

"Yes!" the little girl cried. "And don't use my word."

"Daphne, I'm only trying to protect us, all of us. Can't you see what has been happening since we moved in with Granny? I accidentally killed the giant. I nearly got Mr. Canis killed when the school exploded—and look what's happening to him. Puck had his wings torn off trying to protect me and now Cobweb is dead, too. I'm jinxed. I'm not meant to be a Grimm. Everyone I'm close to is in danger, including you."

"That's crazy talk," the little girl whispered.

"I don't even want to be a fairy-tale detective. Neither did Dad, and when he had his opportunity to walk away, he took it. He did it because he thought this life was too dangerous and he was right. I don't want my sister to get killed or fall under some twisted nutcase's magical spell. I want us to get out now while we still can. If Mom had done the same thing, who knows how our lives would be."

"Our mother was trying to help people," Daphne said. "So she failed. I'd rather try and fail than stand by and watch people suffer. We're Grimms. That's what we *really* do. Help people."

"Daphne, I—"

"I'm getting out of here with or without you, Sabrina," Daphne said. She turned her back on her sister and grew very still. Sabrina knew her well enough to know that talking was over for the night. She only wished that her sister could see her point of view. She had been a "jerkazoid" in the past, but this time she was truly thinking of someone other than herself. With her free hand, she reached for her coat at the end of her bed, searched its pockets, and found her mom's wallet. She opened it up and found the picture she had grown to adore. She stared into her mother's face, unsure of whom Veronica Grimm really was. How could she be so close to her and not know anything about her? Why did Veronica choose this life? Why wouldn't anyone, given the choice, just walk away?

• • •

Smirt woke them early and seemed to enjoy the fact that the girls were exhausted. She unlocked their handcuffs and dragged them out of bed and into the orphanage's kitchen, where they were put to work on the morning breakfast, a disturbing combination of powdered eggs and milk that had a questionable expiration date. A hulking man, who had hairnets on both his head and beard, instructed them to add whatever he handed them out of the fridge to the mix. Several catfish went into the pot—heads, bones, eyes, and all. Next, a bottle of barbecue sauce, a greasy package of bologna, and some mushrooms that might have been picked out of the orphanage's basement.

When all the ingredients were added, the girls were given a

huge wooden spoon, nearly as big as an oar, and told to stir the concoction until it boiled. Every couple of seconds a bubble would appear on the surface of the mix and pop, shooting out a hot spray of steam that scalded their hands. It was hard on Sabrina, but not nearly as hard as Daphne's silence. She tried to talk to her sister several times and the girl just turned away. Deep down she wished for a "snot" or "jerkazoid," but the little girl refused to even insult her.

When "breakfast" was ready, the girls were required to serve it to all the dirty, half-asleep children who staggered through the meal line. There were many faces Sabrina recognized, kids who would probably be in the orphanage until they were old enough to get jobs. None of them seemed to care that the Grimm sisters had returned except for Harold Dink. Harold was a freckle-faced kid with a skin condition that resembled the mange; many patches of his bright red hair were missing. When he got to the counter he sneered, pointed, and laughed. "Hey, everybody! Look! The Sisters Ugly are right back where they started."

"You know, Harold, you should really be nice to the people who are serving you breakfast. You never know what might accidentally fall into your eggs," Daphne said.

"You don't have the guts, geek."

Even though Daphne wasn't speaking to her, Sabrina

instinctively came to her defense. "Hey Harold! Why don't you go steal some more money out of Smirt's office and then pretend you found it for her? How did that turn out the last time? Didn't she send you to live in a petting zoo?"

The kids in line roared with laughter. Harold slammed down his tray and stomped away.

Sabrina and Daphne were the last ones allowed to eat, though neither had much of an appetite for what was left at the bottom of the pot. Instead, they grabbed a couple slices of stale bread and found a table in the back of the cafeteria. Sabrina took a bite of her bread and cringed. It was as tough as cardboard.

"I suppose we're going to meet Greeley today," she said. But despite their united assault on Harold, Daphne didn't respond. Defeated, Sabrina went back to her bread and munched as quietly as she could.

• • •

David Greeley was a skinny guy with stringy muscles and thin chicken legs. His face could have used a shave two weeks earlier, and he had a crooked smile to match his crooked teeth. His forearms were covered in tattoos, many of which looked as if they had been done while riding a horse.

"Yo!" he said when he met them on the front steps of the orphanage.

"Say hello to your new daddy," Ms. Smirt said as she reached down and gave the girls one of her trademark pinches on the shoulder.

Sabrina nodded at their new foster father, but Daphne said nothing.

"Good, they're quiet. Nothing worse than a couple of yapping kids," the man said. "I had a neighbor who had a dog that made a lot of noise. He ain't got no dog no more if you know what I mean." Greeley made a gesture as if he were cocking a shotgun.

Daphne crinkled up her nose and looked as if she was preparing to kick the man in the shins. Sabrina stopped her with a warning hand on the shoulder.

Greeley bent over and rubbed the girls' heads as if they were beagles. "Let's get some things straight, girls. I'm in charge. I don't take no guff and I don't give no guff."

"What does *guff* mean?" Daphne asked.

Sabrina shrugged.

"It means lip, sass, back talk," Greeley answered. "I'm your father now and as your father I deserve a little respect. You do what I say without question and things will go smooth. You don't do what I say then we're going to have problems. There's only one way to do things—my way or the highway."

"So, just to be clear, you want us to do what you tell us to do,"

Sabrina said, though she knew the sarcasm was lost on Greeley. He nodded and smiled. Smirt, on the other hand, gave her another painful pinch.

"It's important to be firm," Ms. Smirt said. "Tough love might just be what these girls need."

"Yeah, so, you said I was going to get some cash for this," Greeley said.

"Yes, your assistance check will come in the mail in seven to ten days," Smirt replied.

Greeley frowned and spit something brown onto the ground. "Well, there goes Atlantic City, doesn't it? Come on, kids. I just got out of the joint and haven't seen my old lady in years. If she plays her cards right she might be your new mommy."

Sabrina took her sister's hand and allowed Mr. Greeley to lead them to his pickup truck.

"Don't come back, girls," Ms. Smirt said with a wicked smile.

The girls climbed into Greeley's truck and he gunned the engine, then whipped it into fourth gear and let the wheels spin until they burned tracks on the ground. He chuckled to himself as if proud of this display, then shifted back into first gear.

"All right, let's get into some trouble," he said.

He drove through the city with reckless abandon. He made turns that were far too dangerous for the amount of snow on the ground and cut people off with glee. He ran several red lights and swore at everyone he saw. He turned one corner and hit a patch of slushy snow, showering water and filth on an old man with a cane. Then he blasted his horn and laughed.

"That was mean!" Daphne shouted.

"That's why it was funny," Greeley said.

"You should go back and see if he's OK."

"Yeah right, kid. I'm not going back to check on that old fool. You don't go back to help someone if you meant to hurt them. He'd beat me to death with his walking stick. Don't you know nothing?"

"What did you just say?" Sabrina asked. "About not going back."

"I said you never go back. What would I say? I'm not sorry? You only go back if you want to help."

Greeley's words echoed in Sabrina's head. *You don't go back to help someone if you meant to hurt them.*

"Daphne, Cobweb didn't kill Oberon!" Sabrina cried.

Daphne turned to her sister. "What?"

"He came back to check on us. He thought we might have been hurt. In fact, he came back twice. Those aren't the actions of a guilty person."

"What the heck are you two babbling about?" Greeley asked.

Sabrina ignored him. "He was worried about us."

"But Oberon told us that Cobweb killed him," Daphne argued. "Do you think he was lying?"

"No, yes, I mean, I don't know. Oberon was a lunatic but there are other things that don't add up. Both Oberon and Cobweb said they had never heard of the Scarlet Hand. Then how did their mark get on the king's body?" Sabrina asked.

"Someone else must have put it there," Daphne said. "Then why did Oberon think Cobweb was the killer?"

"Cobweb was the last person the king saw before he died. He brought him some wine to celebrate their plans. What if someone put the poison in the wine before Cobweb even got it?"

"Hey! Why don't you go back to the no-talky-talky that you were doing when we met. You're givin' me a migraine," Greeley complained.

"We've got to find Granny," Daphne said.

The car stopped at a red light and before Sabrina knew what was happening, Daphne had jumped out of the car, dragging Sabrina with her. The girls had pulled this trick a dozen times but Sabrina had always taken the lead. This time Daphne was doing it and Sabrina was completely unprepared. She fell on the icy pavement as Greeley threw his door open and ran after them screaming, "You come back here!"

Daphne raced ahead, seemingly unaware that Sabrina had fallen. Before the older girl could get to her feet, she felt Greeley's hands in her long blonde hair. He was yanking her up by it.

"Let's go get your sister," he said, pulling her along with one hand and carrying a crowbar in the other. They crossed a busy street, dodging cars and pedestrians, then zipped into an alley. Unfortunately, Daphne had led them all into a dead end. Sabrina watched her sister spin around in panic.

"I thought you were right behind me," Daphne cried. "I'm sorry."

Greeley dragged Sabrina into the alley and tossed her at her sister's feet. Then he smacked his crowbar into the palm of his hand. It made a sickening sound.

"What did I say? What did I say?" he growled. "I said it's my way or the highway."

"I guess we took the highway," Sabrina said, rubbing her sore head.

"Now we've got a problem," Greeley said. "You see, I've got me a temper and when I get angry I do things I regret."

"Don't take another step toward us!" Sabrina shouted.

"See, this is what I'm talking about. I don't want no guff, you little brat," Greeley said. "Didn't they tell you I'd killed seven people?"

"Is that all?" a voice said from above. Sabrina looked up and saw a huge figure dropping out of the sky. He landed on the ground hard, cracking the cement underneath him. When he stood, Sabrina smiled. It was Mr. Canis. "Hardly a number I'd brag about."

Greeley took a step back but then clenched his fists. "Where did you come from? OK, you want to get in my business?" He swung his crowbar threateningly.

"I know *I* want to get into your business," another voice said from behind the thug. It was Mr. Hamstead.

"I was thinking I'd like to as well," a third voice said from above. It was Bess, floating down from the sky with her rocket pack blasting. She touched down on the ground and the flame went out.

"What are you people?" Greeley screamed.

"We're fairy tales," Mr. Hamstead said. "It's time for your bedtime story."

Hamstead punched Greeley in the face, and the greasy criminal fell over like a tree. Bess walked over and kicked the man as he curled up into a ball. Mr. Canis, on the other hand, stood by looking bored. Sabrina could have watched the beating all day but a hand was on her shoulder. She turned and found Granny Relda standing behind her. Daphne was hugging the old woman with all her might but Granny still had a free hand to pull Sabrina into the embrace.

"Come along, girls, we need to leave the city as quickly as possible. I'm afraid I may have gotten the family into a lot of trouble with this incident," Granny replied. "Smirt will surely send the police to arrest me for kidnapping."

"No, Granny, we have to go see Titania," Sabrina said.

"What? Why?"

"She needs to know Cobweb didn't kill her husband."

• • •

When they reached the Golden Egg, Mustardseed was waiting outside Oberon's old office. He led them into the room, where the queen sat solemnly at her husband's desk. She was now wearing a smart pin-striped suit, tailored for her figure but reminiscent of the one Oberon had worn. She had a framed photo in her hands. She looked tired and her eyes were red, as if she had been crying. Oz stood by, watching her with concern. When he noticed the group he rushed to join them.

"Mustardseed, your mother is having a difficult day," he said. "I'm sure I can handle any of this business for her."

"No," Titania said without looking up. "Step forward, son, and bring your friends."

Mustardseed led the family forward and then bowed to his mother.

"This was a happy day," she said holding up the photograph. "We walked through Central Park, amongst the humans. I thought we'd have an eternity of those moments. Now he's gone and there are so many things I wish I had said."

Titania was quiet for a moment. Though Sabrina was bursting to tell her what she had discovered, she knew that silence was the best thing she could offer the heartbroken queen just then.

"I'm told that my husband's murderer has been killed," Titania continued. "Your family's reputation for excellent detective work has proved true."

"We owe you a debt of gratitude," Mustardseed added.

"Actually we have our doubts about Cobweb," Granny said.

"Indeed?" Oz said.

"My granddaughter has given this some serious thought and has some interesting questions that don't have answers," the old woman said, gesturing for Sabrina to step forward.

"You are Puck's chosen protector, I understand," Titania said.

Sabrina nodded, sniffing her still-pungent hair. "For better or worse."

"You don't believe that Cobweb killed his father?" Titania said as Moth entered the room. The fairy girl flashed Sabrina her usual angry look.

Sabrina shook her head. "Cobweb didn't act like a murderer. First, he was working with Oberon to rebuild Faerie. He told me that he and the king were working on a homeless shelter and a hospital. He told me that he respected and supported Oberon."

"He was lying, fool!" Moth cried.

"Sure, a person can say anything, but what they do is different. We chased him all over town. When we were nearly killed in the subway he came back to check on us. Then when the pirates kidnapped us he came to try to rescue us."

"Not the acts of a murderer," Mustardseed said.

Sabrina nodded. "We think it was someone in the Scarlet Hand. No one here seems to know who they are, but back in Ferryport Landing they've caused a lot of trouble. They're responsible for kidnapping my parents and want to take over the world. They left their mark on Oberon's body."

"But you have no idea who this other murderer might be?" Moth asked.

"No," Granny Relda added.

"Then you are no further along toward discovering his killer than when you started!" Titania cried.

Granny stepped forward. "Not exactly. Cobweb gave your husband a glass of wine with poison in it. If we can find out who poured that wine, I believe we'll know who the true killer is."

The queen shook her head. "And how do you propose to learn that?"

"The same way we learned who gave Oberon the poison," Sabrina said.

"Scrooge!" Daphne cried. "He talks to ghosts."

"We can go to see him again and this time we'll talk to Cobweb's spirit," Sabrina explained. "You could come, too. You could talk to Oberon."

Titania rose from her chair. "Is this true?"

Sabrina nodded. "I seem to have the ability to let ghosts take over my body. It's no picnic, but I'd let it happen again so you can tell him a few of those things you never got a chance to say."

"Mother, I've heard talk of Scrooge's talents," Mustardseed said. "Suppose the girl is right. Suppose Cobweb is not the true killer. If that is true, the murderer still walks amongst us. Cobweb could reveal his name."

Titania nodded. "Take me to Scrooge. I'll need a few moments to prepare."

Mustardseed smiled and turned to the group. "We'll join you in the restaurant."

Sabrina and her friends left the office and headed back down the hallway. Moth stopped them and sighed as if she were exhausted. She looked at Sabrina and gritted her teeth.

"Puck could emerge at any moment from his vessel. As his protector, it is customary for you to perform a sacred task."

"What kind of task?" Sabrina asked.

"You must toast the emerging king with a special elixir. It is quite an honor."

"I really can't," Sabrina argued. "We're leaving any minute. Can it wait?"

"I also thought you would like some time alone with Puck. He's the King of Faerie now. If the kingdom is to be rebuilt, he will have a great deal of responsibility. He'll have to stay in the city."

Sabrina felt something rise into her throat and realized it was her heart. She had never given any thought to the idea that Puck might not come home with them. But of course he would stay. He was a king now, and why would he go back to Ferryport Landing and be trapped inside the town again? She suddenly felt the need to cry, then laughed out loud. *Cry?* Puck was an irritating pain in the behind. He was constantly giving her a hard time, putting slimy things in her bed, dumping her into big vats of sticky glop. There had never been a meal he didn't ruin with his explosive flatulence. She should be happy to get rid of him. She would be free of his army of chimpanzees, his pranks, his name calling. But then, there had been the kiss. Her first kiss. Their first kiss . . .

"I think we have a few minutes," Granny Relda said.

"OK," Sabrina said. "I'll do it."

Moth led her down the hallway to her room. Once inside, the little fairy closed the door and locked it. "No one can enter during the ceremony."

Puck's cocoon was inside what looked like a giant birdcage, and the second Sabrina stepped toward it the cocoon slammed against the bars, seemingly in an effort to be near her.

"I will prepare the elixir," Moth said.

"You do that," Sabrina said, impatiently.

Moth came to a table filled with potions and powders and went to work, busily mixing them together in a small, ceramic cup.

"On the day of a fairy's emergence from its cocoon, our people drink a ceremonial toast to a healthy new life. Very few humans have ever been present," Moth said.

"Well, I'm happy to be included," Sabrina said, reaching into the cage and putting her hand on the slimy cocoon. She expected it to be cold and damp like before but it was warm and alive. Maybe he could hear her.

"Puck, I've come to say good-bye. You're free from Ferryport Landing. That's something a lot of Everafters and I, myself, would like to be. You're going to stay here with your mother and brother. Apparently, you're the new king of the fairies so you're going to have to grow up a little. I . . . I never got a chance to say I was sorry for slugging you when you . . . you . . . well you know." The memory of their kiss flashed into her mind again. "I wasn't expecting it and, well, it wasn't exactly a dream come true to be surrounded by a bunch of tick-eating chimpanzees. I was angry when it happened. But, I'm glad it was you."

She could feel tears welling up in her eyes. "OK, enough of that. You take care of yourself. I'm going to come back here someday and if I find out you were a jerkazoid, there's going to be trouble."

Moth returned with two goblets. She handed one to Sabrina and raised it for a toast. "To Puck."

"To Puck." Sabrina took a drink. Whatever the ceremonial elixir was it didn't taste half-bad. There was a fruity taste like raspberries, but there was also a hint of honey and oatmeal, and there was something else, something a little bitter that she couldn't quite place.

"So, I suppose you two will be getting married," Sabrina said conversationally.

"Naturally. Once Puck learns that it was I who brought his father's killer to justice, he'll of course take me as his bride. I needed to prove I was worthy of him."

"Well, don't forget to send me an invitation to the big day," Sabrina said with a sneer.

Moth flashed one back at her.

"To be honest, Princess, I wouldn't be surprised if he didn't show up back on our front porch," Sabrina said taking another sip of her drink. "He seems to enjoy tormenting me."

Moth set down her glass. "I thought the same thing."

Suddenly, there was a horrible pain in Sabrina's belly. It was so powerful she doubled over. She lost her breath and fought to catch it as a second wave of pain rolled over her. She fell to her knees. The goblet of elixir tumbled onto the floor and spilled its contents all over the boards.

"Moth, I'm sick. Go get my grandmother!" Sabrina cried.

"You think you've got his heart, don't you, human? Well, it's something you should have never had and I'm taking it back."

Sabrina looked down at the cup. Had Moth put something in it? Everything was so confusing, and the pain was so intense, like someone stabbing her with a hot knife.

"Imagine my humiliation when Puck rejected me! Imagine the looks people gave me! I was supposed to be the next queen! But I held my head high and hoped he would change his mind. But he never got a chance! His father had him thrown out of the kingdom."

"Get help," Sabrina grunted.

"When you brought him back I thought Oberon would give him another chance, but he refused. He told the guards that as soon as Puck was well he was to be removed. So, I had to act fast. I snatched Cobweb's pouch when he wasn't looking and mixed some potions and powders. I collected it in a bottle and stepped back into the celebration. There was food, wine, everything one needs for a proper feast. Cobweb ran past me with a goblet of wine. I knew it was for the king. Cobweb was a loyal and attentive servant. I distracted him and poured the potion into the cup. Moments later, Oberon was dead. I couldn't believe my luck, but then you and your family had to get involved and then Puck chose you as his protector! I was humiliated, again. Well, human, this time I'm not going to let anything get in my way."

Another stab of pain hit Sabrina in the belly. This time, it migrated up her spine toward her brain. She could barely think straight and she was too weak to fight back or even call out for help. But there was something going on in the birdcage. Had she just seen Puck's cocoon change shape?

"Cobweb will tell the truth," Sabrina groaned.

"Not without you," Moth reminded her. "That old fool Scrooge couldn't get his grandmother to call from the beyond. I'll just tell your family you decided to stay here for Puck's emergence while they go ghost hunting. Even if Cobweb does manage to communicate without you, I've made enough elixir for your entire family, Titania, and Mustardseed."

Sabrina heard a ripping sound. Or had it been her imagination? It was becoming difficult to focus.

"Now that Puck is king we are going to rebuild Faerie, right here. I've already mapped out most of Central Park. We'll run the humans out and build a proper castle. Then we'll show the rest of the Everafters who's in charge. They'll bow at our feet."

That ripping sound again. It was coming from behind Moth.

"Then we'll take over the whole city. Humans will make good slaves," Moth continued.

Sabrina lifted her heavy eyelids and saw a familiar figure looking down on her from behind Moth.

"Grimm, are you in trouble again? I swear, if I had a nickel for every time I had to save your sorry behind I'd be a rich fairy."

"Puck," she groaned.

"Your Majesty," Moth said as she spun around. "I can explain this—"

But she never finished her sentence. Puck took out his flute and blasted a couple of notes. A stream of pixies soared through the window, swooped down, and lifted Sabrina off the ground.

"What did you do to her, Moth?"

The little princess shook her head. "You don't understand, my love. I did this for us."

Puck noticed the goblet lying on the floor. He picked it up and smelled it. "Now that wasn't very nice."

Puck turned to his pixies. "Find Cobweb. We need his medicine."

There was some buzzing and Puck's face curled up in horror. "My father?"

The pixies twittered on.

"Then half of you find my mother. The other half keep an eye on the princess."

The pixies did as they were told, depositing Sabrina in Puck's arms as they set about their tasks. Puck raced to the locked door and transformed his legs into those of an elephant. He used one to kick open the door and it flew off its hinges and into the hallway. Sabrina looked back to see Moth swatting wildly at the little dots of light.

Sabrina was starting to feel cold. She trembled so forcefully it hurt. And then the world started to grow very dim. She could hear Puck telling her to stay awake but she couldn't. She was so tired. She just wanted to rest. Maybe if she did the pain would go away.

She had a disorienting dream. Puck was standing over her, but he quickly morphed into Titania, who melted into Granny Relda and then into Daphne, who was crying. *Don't cry, Daphne.* Then Daphne became Canis, who became Hamstead, who became Bess, who became black nothingness.

• • •

Sabrina woke up in the dark. No, *dark* wasn't the right word. There was light but it was faint and seemed to be behind the walls of the tiny room she was sitting in. No, *room* wasn't the right word, either. It was a space, something small, something confined. She tried to stretch out but her hands met a cold, damp wall. She reached down and realized she was sitting in fluid, something like gravy, and it was halfway up her chest. She started to panic, reaching around for an opening, and found something above her like a seam. She pushed upward and a small portion of it tore away. A bright light flooded the space and she forced herself to stand. She had freed herself and there, waiting on the other side, was her family.

"That was the most disgusting thing I've ever seen," Puck said. "Why don't I carry a camera with me?"

Sabrina looked down at the prison she had just escaped from and quickly fought the urge to barf when she realized she had just been inside her own cocoon. Granny Relda and Oz rushed to her and wiped away the layers of goop.

"How are you feeling?" Granny asked.

"I feel fine, though I'll never eat eggplant again as long as I live," Sabrina said, looking down at the crushed cocoon.

"The cocoon removed the poisons from your system and allowed you to heal," Oz explained. "What Moth used would have been lethal without it."

"She tried to poison you like she did Oberon," Daphne said, rushing to her sister and wrapping her arms around Sabrina's neck. "The pixies made her confess."

"She told me everything," Sabrina said. "She was trying to impress Puck. She was hoping to prove herself so he would marry her. Where is she?"

"She has been arrested. She'll see a judge as soon as we can determine who might be qualified to be one," Mustardseed said. He smiled and turned to his brother. "Mom's waiting."

"Duty calls," Puck said as he rolled his eyes. He waved to Sabrina and left with his brother.

Granny hugged Sabrina and burst into tears. "I am sorry, Sabrina. I would never forgive myself if you got hurt. I should protect you. I should prevent any harm from happening to you."

"This wasn't your fault," Sabrina replied. "We knew Moth was mean, we just didn't know she was homicidal. We need to question her about the Scarlet Hand now. She can tell us things.

She might even know who kidnapped Mom and Dad and put the spell on them."

Granny shook her head. "She confessed to everything. She isn't in the Scarlet Hand."

9

n Christmas Eve morning, Sabrina, Daphne, Granny Relda, Mr. Canis, Mr. Hamstead, Bess, Mustardseed, Puck, Titania, Oz, and a slew of fairies stood on a desolate bank of the Hudson River. On the shore was a boat carved from the trunk of an enormous tree. Inside, Oberon's body rested, gently rising and falling with the river's waves. A long sword was in his hands and he was wearing a suit of leather armor with a lion painted on the chest plate.

Titania gave a speech, wishing her husband a safe passage into the next world. She placed a red rose on his chest, which she said had been grown in the fairy homeland, and then she stepped aside. Mustardseed followed, sharing memories of his father: his bravery in days long ago, his struggles as Faerie's new home in America collapsed, and even his plans to rebuild. He placed a white rose next to his mother's red. Then it was Puck's turn to speak.

"My father was a complicated man—one of strong traditions. He had unbendable beliefs and those beliefs often got in the way of new beginnings. He wanted the best for us but he didn't always know how to make that happen, and he was easily frustrated when we disagreed. As I am the new King of Faerie, his blood will endure."

Puck tossed a green rose onto his father's chest. One of the ogres from the Golden Egg stepped forward with a torch and handed it to Puck. The boy fairy took it and set the boat ablaze. Then he and his brother pushed it out into the water. The flames quickly engulfed the floating casket and the river took it away. Soon, it was out of sight.

Oz stepped up to the Ferryport Landing group. "I suppose you'll be leaving soon."

Granny Relda nodded. "We've got to get back home and see if we can wake up the girls' parents."

"I wish you the best of luck," Oz said as he turned to the girls and shook their hands. "Well, I've got to get back to work. It's Christmas Eve and another one of the elves is on the fritz."

The crowd began to drift away. Granny suggested they return to their hotel for some rest before the long drive home. Sabrina said she'd be along in a minute and then turned back toward Puck. He was discussing something with his brother. Mustardseed nodded and his wings popped out of his back. He took to the sky and flew away.

Sabrina walked over to join Puck. He didn't notice her at first but when he did he quickly wiped his tears on his sleeve. He forced a smile but then let it fade. She reached out and took his hand and they stood looking out at the river in silence.

"So, what do I call you? Your Majesty?"

"You should have been calling me that all along," Puck said.

"What you said was very nice," Sabrina said.

"My mother wrote it for me. She didn't care too much for what I came up with myself."

Sabrina smiled. "There's no one here now. Why don't you go ahead with your version?"

Puck tilted his head curiously at Sabrina and smiled.

"My father was mean, arrogant, horrible, and selfish. He cared little for anyone and less for those who disagreed with him. His only love was for his precious kingdom."

Sabrina raised her eyebrows, admiring the boy's honesty, but remained quiet.

Puck turned to the water as if his father were still there, listening.

"I hated you!" he shouted. "You took every opportunity to remind me that I was weak and stupid!"

Suddenly, Puck fell to his knees. Tears streamed down his cheeks. Sabrina rushed to him, knelt down, and used her scarf to wipe them away.

"When I was barely out of diapers he took me aside and told me I would never be king. He said I was a disappointment to him and he would never give up his throne to me. I went to my mother in tears and she explained him to me. She said he was worried about the kingdom's future and feared that his successor would destroy it—even if that successor was his own son. But my mother swore that one day I would wear the crown, and he would never see it coming. Until then, I would have my own kingdom. Then she gave me my name: the Trickster King. I've worn it proudly ever since.

"When I got older he tried to force me to marry Moth. So I told the old man he was nuts. Disobeying your father is a crime in our world. He banished me. But, here I am, the King of Faerie anyway. My mother was right. He never saw it coming."

He stood up and wiped his eyes on his sleeve. "If you tell anyone I was crying, you'll regret it, pus-brain."

"I won't tell, stinkpot," Sabrina said affectionately. "Looks like you and me finally have something in common."

"What's that?"

"Families we're not sure we want to be part of," Sabrina replied.

"The old lady told me you're quitting," Puck said.

"I'm not quitting. I'm retiring. You can't quit something you never wanted to do in the first place," Sabrina said defensively.

"You can't quit something you never tried either."

"I tried! But people got hurt when I tried," Sabrina said. "Look at Mr. Canis, and you!"

"Oh, poor Sabrina. Such a walking disaster. I was there. Mr. Canis didn't get hurt because you were being stupid. You were the one that saved him, and the rest of us. If you hadn't done what you did we'd all be dead. The truth is, and I hate to admit it, but you're a hero and a pretty good one. You help people when no one else can. From what I hear that's what your mother did, too. It's in your blood, and blood isn't something you can walk away from."

"When did you suddenly become Mister Maturity?"

Puck laughed. "Don't worry. It won't last." Then he belched in her face. "See! It's over."

"So, I guess you're going to have to stay and take over what's left of Faerie," Sabrina said softly.

Before Puck could answer, there was a loud commotion up on the hill overlooking the river. People were shouting and screaming. Puck and Sabrina looked at each other and then ran to find out what was going on.

Mr. Hamstead was lying on the ground. Bess knelt beside him. Tony Fats was hovering above the couple with clenched fists. Poor Mr. Hamstead looked as if he had been socked in the eye.

"I told you to leave my girl alone!" Tony Fats yelled.

"And I told you I'm not your girl anymore, Tony!" Bess cried.

Mr. Hamstead crawled to his feet. "Bess, I can handle this." He turned to Tony Fats. "Is this how you want to do it? That's fine with me."

The two men rushed at each other, throwing fists and landing horrible blows. Tony Fats was the first to fall but he quickly got up and knocked Mr. Hamstead into a mud puddle. The portly man fell with a painful thud.

Sabrina spotted Mr. Canis in the crowd. He was watching as if he had no concern for his friend. Sabrina raced to him and tugged on his sleeve. "We have to stop this. Mr. Hamstead is going to get hurt."

Mr. Canis shook his head. "The pig is tougher than he looks, child."

"Tony Fats is twice his size!" Sabrina cried.

"And the Wolf is four times his size and Hamstead had no trouble taking me down. As I said, he's tougher than he looks."

Tony Fats kicked Hamstead mercilessly, forcing him to flounder in the mud. Each time their friend tried to get up, Tony attacked, keeping him on his hands and knees.

"You don't come to my town and steal my girl!" Tony Fats bellowed. "You don't know who you're messing with."

"Leave him alone, Tony!" Bess demanded.

Tony's face twisted into a demented smile. "I've got to teach your friend here how we do it in the big city." He lifted his leg to deliver another nasty kick, but this time Hamstead caught it. He pulled hard and Tony Fats fell onto his back. Hamstead leaped onto him and the two men wrestled for dominance.

Then, all at once, Sabrina saw a magic wand appear in Tony Fats's hand.

"Hamstead, look out!" Canis roared.

Mr. Hamstead must have spotted the wand himself as he sent an elbow into Tony's gut. The fairy godfather let out a wheeze and dropped the wand but then scampered to get it back. Hamstead was right on top of him and the two fought for control over the weapon. They rolled around in the mud, struggling viciously. But just as Mr. Hamstead gained the upper hand, a transformation came over him. His arms and legs suddenly shrank into stubby hoofed feet. His clothes disappeared and his pink skin blanched white. His ears migrated up his head and turned into furry points. In a matter of seconds Mr. Hamstead's true form was revealed. He was a pig.

But he was a pig with a magic wand in his snout. He flicked his head in a circle and a beam of magic shot out of the starry tip. It hit Tony Fats. There was a puff of smoke, and when it disappeared the big fairy godfather was gone, replaced with a beady-eyed rat. The rat twittered, sized up the enormous pig hovering over him, shrieked, and then raced off, disappearing over the hill.

"I told you so," Mr. Canis mumbled.

Sabrina nodded. She had to admit Mr. Hamstead was a lot more resourceful than she had ever given him credit for being. Daphne raced to the enormous pig and gave him a big hug around the neck.

"I'm so proud of you, Mr. Hamstead," the little girl said.

"Ernie?" a voice said from behind them. The pig looked up and Sabrina followed his gaze. Bess was standing there, looking confused and shocked. "Ernie, you're a . . ."

"Pig." Mr. Hamstead had suddenly morphed back to his human form. He looked as if he wanted to be a million miles away. "I'm a pig, Bess. One of the Three Little Pigs. I should have told you. It wasn't fair. I'm sorry."

Hamstead turned abruptly, pushed his way through the crowd, and disappeared.

"Ernie!" Bess cried after him, but he was gone.

"We should go get him," Daphne said to her grandmother.

"No, *liebling*," Granny said sadly. "He needs some time to himself."

• • •

When they got back to the hotel, Mr. Canis decided to meditate while they waited for Hamstead to show up. The old man was sure the traffic out of town would test his temper. Granny bought a suitcase so they could pack the few things the family had purchased during their stay in the city. While they packed they enjoyed a big lunch, compliments of room service. Puck, who had come to see them off, spent most of the afternoon talking to the numerous pixies who visited at the hotel window. He gave them several orders and answered their questions, and they raced off to do his bidding. King Puck was already hard at work.

Sabrina slipped into the bathroom for some privacy. She washed her face, brushed her teeth, and studied herself in the mirror. She had her father's golden hair and blue eyes, but her face was Veronica's. She knew when she was older she would look a lot like her mother.

But as her mother's features stared back at her, she wondered why she hadn't gotten more of her mother's spirit. Why had

Veronica chosen to take on the family responsibility? Why had she chosen such a dangerous life? If only Veronica were awake and Sabrina could ask her.

She took her mother's pink wallet out of her pocket and opened it. Inside was the picture of Veronica, Sabrina, and Daphne. Next to it was the business card of her mother's best friend, Oz Diggs, also known as the Wonderful Wizard of Oz— a man who claimed to know her better than anyone. And suddenly Sabrina had an idea.

She burst out of the bathroom and found Daphne and Puck finishing off three huge hot fudge sundaes. "I want to talk to Oz," Sabrina said to her grandmother.

"Sabrina, we should get on the road as soon as rush hour is over. I thought you wanted to get back home so you could help wake up your mother and father," Granny said.

"This is about my mother and father," Sabrina said. "Please! I need to ask him some questions. I need to understand my mother."

• • •

Sabrina, Daphne, Granny Relda, and Puck took a taxi down to Thirty-fourth Street. It was evening by the time they reached Macy's and there was a steady stream of exhausted shoppers flooding out of the doors, but the family managed to squirm their way inside. The store security guard blocked their path, frowned, and tapped his watch. "Christmas Eve, folks. We're closing in five minutes."

"We're not buying anything. We're looking for the Wizard," Sabrina said.

"The who?"

"We're looking for Mr. Diggs," Granny interrupted.

"He's probably in his workroom," the guard grumbled. "Just don't dillydally, all right? Some of us would like to go home."

They found Oz's workroom. Sabrina knocked once and waited patiently for several minutes, but no one answered.

"C'mon," Puck said as he opened the door and pushed Sabrina inside.

"Children, we are intruding," Granny worried.

"He might be in the back and can't hear us," Daphne said, pulling the old woman inside.

The room was as big of a mess as the first time they had seen it. Several tables had parts on them that were still moving, including a head that kept opening its eyes and lifting its brows in surprise. Tools were scattered around the room, some of them seeming to have found permanent homes on the floor.

"Ugh, do you smell that?" Puck asked.

"No. What are you talking about?" Sabrina said defensively.

She thought the cocoon smell had finally faded but worried that maybe she was just getting used to it.

"Hard work, I smell hard work in here. It's horrible," Puck said as he picked up a circuit board and examined it. "I might gag."

"Oz?" Sabrina called out, but there was no answer, only the buzz of electric engines. "Oz, I want to ask you about my mother."

"Perhaps we should sit and wait for him," Granny said.

Sabrina hoped the security guards wouldn't lock them inside, but she took her grandmother's advice and sat down on a stool. When Daphne did the same, a robotic head that was sitting on the table next to her sprang to life and started giggling. The little girl screamed and snatched a hammer off the table, then smacked the head a couple times until it stopped laughing.

"Uh, relax," Sabrina said.

"You taught him a lesson, didn't you, marshmallow?" Puck said as he took the hammer from the little girl. He hit the head himself for good measure and scanned the room for something else to beat on. After awhile, he sat down and started peeking through a stack of papers on the desk.

"Don't snoop," Granny Relda scolded.

"Then someone better keep me entertained 'cause this is boring," Puck replied.

Sabrina got up and took the papers away from the fairy. "This is his stuff. Some of it might be private." She tried to collect them in a neat stack, but shoved in the middle of the pile was something quite different: a small, leather-bound journal with gold writing on its cover.

Fairy Tale Accounts
June 1992 to present
Veronica Grimm

Sabrina felt her heart rocking in her chest. With trembling fingers she picked up the book and opened it.

"What did you find?" Granny Relda said.

"It's my mother's journal," Sabrina replied. Veronica's curvy, slightly sloppy script filled every page. There were hundreds of entries chronicling her experiences with the Everafters of both Ferryport Landing and New York City. Sabrina read feverishly, turning pages faster and faster, absorbing as much as she could about her mother's secret life. There was story after story of the lives she had changed. She had helped people move, find jobs, and track down missing friends, and she had done plenty of detective work as well. On one of the pages she wrote:

My work with these people is exciting, fascinating, and most of all—important. I've found that there is more to being a Grimm than Henry ever told me. It's more than being a detective . . . sometimes, I'm the only hope an Everafter has of making it in this world. If only I could get them to work together . . .

Sabrina flipped to the back and found several folded pages from a yellow legal pad, covered with writing. She read through them, including all the scratched-out parts and tiny notes in the margins. It was a speech.

"This is the speech everyone was talking about. It was her plan for the Everafters. She was supposed to give it the day she disappeared," Sabrina said.

"Then what is Oz doing with it?" Daphne asked, taking the journal from her sister.

Granny got up from her chair. "*Lieblings,* I think it would be wise of us to—"

A voice from the shadows cut her off. "Oh, I wish you hadn't found that."

Oz stepped into the light. "Your mother was a remarkable woman, Sabrina. She had a charisma that was almost, well, supernatural. She could convince people to do anything she wanted. It was a talent I always envied. Your mother collected an army of supporters using only her smile.

"And I was one of them. I loved the little adventures we used to get into. She was part saint, part detective, and for a long time I thought I wanted to be like her. But then I would come into work every day, and have my boss criticize the displays. I'd go home to my little apartment in Queens and spend the rest of my time holding the hand of King Oberon. And it dawned on me that my life had taken a turn for the worse. I used to be the 'great and terrible Oz!' I was the ruler of an entire nation. People feared me. What had happened?"

"You're talking in circles, Wizard," Puck said, drawing his wooden sword from a loop around his waist.

"Kids—they always want the short version. Fine. One day, I was approached by a man who offered me something more. He promised me that there would come a day when the city would need a leader to rule both Everafter and human alike. So I signed up to be a member of the Scarlet Hand."

Sabrina gasped. "Then *you* killed Oberon. You put the mark on his chest!"

"Oh no, Moth killed him. I just took advantage of the situation in order to announce the coming of my master's army. I put the mark on Oberon's chest when I found him dead, then escaped just before his body was discovered. I'm no murderer."

"But you are a kidnapper. How else would you have my mother's journal?"

"It was part of my deal with the master, Sabrina. In exchange for your parents I get to rule this city."

"And how do you plan on doing that?" Puck asked

"Why, by taking over the world," he said. "The master is attempting nothing short of world domination, and not a minute too soon, either. The humans have had control for long enough. Look at what they've done with their time. The world is a cesspool of pollution, hate, and greed. It's time for the Everafters to start running the show."

"And Henry and Veronica were in the way," Granny Relda said.

"I'm not proud of what I've done but, unfortunately, yes. Veronica was a brilliant, insightful woman with big ideas. She wanted to unite this city under one government. She actually thought these fools could work together. I couldn't allow that. I have to keep this community in chaos until I can claim the city as mine. An organized population of Everafters would be difficult to topple."

"So, you kidnapped my mom and dad! You put them to sleep!" Daphne cried.

"Yes to the first, no to the second. I lured them out, promising your mother I would help her with her speech and encouraging her to reveal her double life to your father. Once I had them, I turned them over to the master. I had no idea they were still alive until you arrived here."

Suddenly, there was a loud bang and the lights went off in the building. The security guards were closing the store.

"Now, about that book. There's a speech inside that I need to get back. You can keep the journal. But no one can ever hear Veronica's speech. You and your family can go back to Ferryport Landing. Your mother and father's usefulness to the master is over and as long as you stay out of the way you'll live. Not a bad trade."

"No chance," Sabrina said.

The Wizard reached into his pocket and removed his small, silver remote. "Then, so be it." He pushed a button and at once every little robot head turned toward them with electrical eyes blazing. The machines that could move charged at them, some dragging half-assembled bodies. Puck swatted a few away with his wooden sword, but one of the mechanical birds swooped down and snatched the journal out of Sabrina's hand. It immediately flew back to Oz and gave him its prize. Then Oz ran.

The family had to fight through the crowd of misfit robots to chase after him as he dashed out of the workroom and through the empty store. It was mostly dark but there were a few security lights on, so it was easy to follow him. But he kept overturning racks of clothing and merchandise in the family's path.

Puck stopped, spun around on his heels, and quickly transformed into a bull with huge horns. He bent his head down, stomped his front hooves a few times, blasted a breath out of his nostrils, and then charged forward, tossing the obstacles out of the way. The women raced close behind.

They watched Oz take the escalator up to the floor above. Puck transformed back to his normal state, then raced up the escalator two stairs at a time. Sabrina wasn't far behind. Daphne stayed back to help Granny along.

They chased Oz up five flights, with Puck still in the lead. They were racing through the sporting goods department when Sabrina saw Puck flail through the air and slam into a nearby wall. Then, something came around the corner at her. Sabrina had seen it many times before as a young girl. She had associated it with sugarplum dreams. Now it made her think of nightmares. It was a seven-foot-tall Nutcracker, painted to look like a red-coated soldier with a white beard. Its most horrible feature was a gaping mouth that smashed closed every few moments as if it were gnashing its teeth.

"Oh dear," Granny said as she and Daphne came up behind Sabrina.

Puck crawled to his feet, rushed behind the Nutcracker, and delivered a well-placed kick to its behind. The robot turned and lunged at him.

"They don't sell explosives in this store, do they?" Puck shouted, as he dodged the creature's massive arm.

"They sell everything else," Sabrina said, glancing at a store directory on the wall. "Wait a minute. Sporting Goods! We're on the sporting goods floor!"

With Puck keeping the monster's attention, she and her family raced around, choosing weapons. Daphne found a tennis racket, which she swung wildly at the robot, but her racket turned into splinters when it got caught in the Nutcracker's deadly jaws. Granny found a couple of soccer balls, but when she raced back to use them on the robot, it easily deflected her blows.

"What's that thing?" Puck said. He was pointing to an odd machine that said PITCHMASTER on the side. The contraption had a pump that shot balls through a tube at super speeds. Sabrina guessed it was to teach batters how to hit fastballs. *Fastballs!*

She flipped the machine on and pushed a button, and a baseball rocketed out of the tube and hit a nearby mannequin, knocking its head off its shoulders.

"Oh, I've got to get me one of those things!" Puck said. "Do you think it will shoot balloons filled with donkey poo?"

Sabrina ignored Puck's disgusting idea and shouted to her sister, "Help me turn this toward the Nutcracker!"

When they had the machine lined up, Sabrina hit the button again and a ball screamed out of the tube and hit the Nutcracker in the chest. The force was so incredible it left a huge dent.

The creature turned, a red light flashing in its mechanical eyes. It rushed at them so quickly, the only thing to do was push the button on the ball machine and hold it down. A ball crashed into the robot's face, knocking a metal panel off and revealing its wiring. Then another slammed into its right leg. Each ball knocked the robot back, but each time it recovered and kept coming at them.

Sabrina quickly studied the pitchmaster's controls. There was a button that read LIGHTNING FASTBALL. She pushed it just as the Nutcracker's hand reached out for her. A ball shot out of the machine's tube and hit the creature between the eyes. Smoke suddenly billowed out of its head, and little sparks of fire popped around inside what had been the robot's brain. A second later the creature fell over and moved no more.

There was a loud clang and Sabrina turned. Oz had been hiding nearby and knocked over a rack of bicycles in his effort to escape. He raced to the escalators and the entire family took off after him. As soon as the Wizard reached the top of one escalator, he hurried to the next until he had quickly reached the of the store. When the Grimms and Puck finally got there, he was nowhere in sight.

"Oz, we know you're up here," Granny Relda called out.

"Yeah, you can't hide from us or from the beating you're going to get when we find you," Puck said.

"Shut up! You're not helping," Sabrina said.

"Don't tell me to shut up. I'm a king," Puck said.

"You're an idiot."

Just then, an enormous glowing head materialized out of thin air. It seemed to be made of emerald-green fire and had horrible black eyes. When its mouth opened, Oz's voice came bellowing out. "I have never had luck with children. I have to admit I've always underestimated them and they have been my undoing."

Puck snatched a giant candy cane decoration off a wall nearby and swung it at the head. "Aw, shut up." The cane passed right through the head, breaking up the image only temporarily.

"Look at Dorothy," the head continued. "That little girl was a moron, I tell you. I mean, dumber than a box of rocks. She comes to me asking for a way back to Kansas. I mean, if you could have a wizard grant a wish, would you waste it on going to Kansas? And her friends! 'Give me a heart!' 'Give me a brain!' 'Give me courage!' What they needed was a clue. So, I sent them to see the Wicked Witch of the West. Who would have thought they'd ever come back? They ruined everything for me. Well, I won't let it happen, again. It's time the Wizard got a wish of his own."

Sabrina motioned for everyone to follow her. Oz had to be hiding somewhere nearby.

"You're not going to get away with this," she muttered.

"Oh, but I am," Oz cried as the head followed her. "After all, I'm the great and terrible Wizard. I can do magic, child, and I've got a lot of tricks up my sleeve."

They turned a corner and found the man standing in plain view. He was busy working the buttons on his silver remote control, pounding them frantically and causing the little device to squeal and honk. When he finally noticed the family, he groaned. "Don't look behind the curtain," he said with an uncomfortable laugh.

"Oz, give me the book," Sabrina said.

"I can't, child," he said. The Wizard shook his head as he pushed a button on his remote, then backed away from the group.

Suddenly there was an incredible rumbling beneath them. The building shifted as a fissure opened up, snaking across the entire floor. Puck and the Grimms were knocked to their knees. The floor was splitting in two to make way for something big, round, and green. It rose higher and higher, and got bigger and bigger, until it nearly filled the entire store. With nowhere else to go, it pushed through the ceiling, causing concrete and wood to crash down around everyone.

"Is this another one of his robots?" Puck shouted as he clung to Sabrina.

"No! It's something else," she said as a large woven basket rose up from below. It was attached to the giant green orb by ropes and had a silver furnace inside it. The Wizard climbed into the basket and then it too lifted upward. Suddenly, Sabrina knew exactly what the thing was. "It's a hot-air balloon."

The basket rose through the hole in the ceiling and the balloon was aloft.

"Give me the journal, Oz!" Sabrina cried.

"Is that the wish you want the mighty Oz to grant?" he cried as he rose higher and higher. "Then you will have to do something for me first."

"Stop playing games!" Granny Relda cried.

"You know the story, people. You can have your heart's desire but you have to do something for me. You have to kill the Wicked Witch of the West!" Sabrina saw Oz push another button on his controller just as the balloon disappeared from sight.

"I don't think he's my favorite anymore," Daphne said.

"I'll get him," Puck cried, beginning to flap his wings; but suddenly there was more loud rumbling from below and he spun around, midair. Sabrina felt it, too. It seemed as if the entire building was being rocked back and forth. Then, all at once, the shaking stopped.

"Uh, what was that?" Sabrina said.

Granny looked around nervously. "I don't know and I don't like it."

The old woman grabbed Daphne and Sabrina by the hands and hurried them over to the emergency exit. Puck flew after them. Together, the group raced down nine flights of stairs.

They finally reached the ground floor of the department store and found it a disaster. Racks of clothing and broken bottles of perfume were scattered over the floor, and hosiery was draped everywhere. Worst of all, an enormous canyon had opened up in the floor.

"Find an exit, children," Granny said. But, before they could take a step, a big, black, metallic cone began to rise out of the breech in the floor. It rose and rose, expanding as it came.

"This can't be good," Puck said.

Soon the enormous cone was completely revealed, but beneath it came another object. This one was also made of metal, though it had a sickly green tint to it. It rose higher and higher, revealing a pair of eyes, one covered in a black patch. Then came a long, pointy, wart-covered nose. Then a mouth with jagged steel fangs. Sabrina knew what was erupting from below. The cone was a hat, and the face was one she'd seen in a book. She grabbed her sister and her grandmother, shook them until they took their eyes off the growing horror, and together with Puck ran for the closest door.

"What is that thing?" Puck shouted.

"It's the Wicked Witch of the West!" Sabrina shouted back. She pushed hard on the door, but it was locked tight. She had forgotten the store was closed. She pounded on the glass, hoping that it would shatter, but she wasn't strong enough. Thankfully, Puck understood the situation. He morphed his arm into that of a gorilla's and punched the door with all his might. Not only did the glass break, but the door flew off its hinges and the family raced out into the snow.

Unfortunately, they were not alone. The streets were packed with people. Taxis, trucks, and cars were everywhere. It was then that Sabrina realized how much easier it was to handle these types of disasters in Ferryport Landing, where the downtown area was usually barren. But here, in New York City, the city that never slept, every corner was as crowded as a parade.

"Run!" Granny Relda yelled, and the family took off down the sidewalk.

"Get off the streets!" Sabrina shouted to the crowd. "There's a monster!"

People ignored her and went about their business, but she still tried to get their attention. "There's a giant robot coming! Run for your lives!"

The family dashed in and out of the crowd and quickly reached the corner of the street. The traffic was intense so they couldn't just run out into it. They were forced to wait for the light, which gave Sabrina a chance to look back at the store. She did so just in time to see the entire front of the building collapse and a huge leg step through. That got the New Yorkers' attention. Cars drove into trucks. A taxi crashed into a newspaper stand.

When the light changed, the family raced across the street, continuing to shout warnings at everyone they saw. Sabrina heard a huge pounding noise and looked back again. The robot was completely free of the store now. It stood nearly six stories tall. It scanned the streets and then fixed its horrible electronic gaze on Sabrina. It began to walk in her direction, kicking a taxicab out of the way. The cab slammed into a light pole and then skidded into the intersection. A truck that had the misfortune of driving near the creature's shoe was knocked aside and sent into a nearby building.

The family kept running, but now the pedestrians were getting smart. Suddenly, the wave they had been fighting against turned, and crowds of New Yorkers ran with them. Many looked back as they ran, and a young woman knocked Daphne to the ground in her panic. Puck swooped up the little girl before she was trampled.

"How are we going to stop this thing?" Puck shouted. "I think it's going to take more than a couple of fastballs."

"Look!" Daphne said, pointing above them. Sabrina saw Oz's hot-air balloon sailing into the sky. It was strangely close to the Empire State Building. In fact, it was too close. The spire at the top had caught the balloon.

"He can stop the witch!" Sabrina shouted. "Head for the Empire State Building!"

The family raced on, but the enormous witch grew closer with each giant step. By the time they got to the skyscraper the robot was right on top of them. They pushed through the revolving doors of the famous building and dashed into the bronze-covered lobby.

A security guard got up from his desk and held up his hand. "We're closed, folks. Come back next week."

"We've got to get to the top now," Sabrina said.

"No can do, people . . ." he said, his voice trailing off. Sabrina realized something had captured his attention. She turned to follow his gaze and saw the witch's good eye staring through the front doors. A second later, its enormous hand smashed through the entrance and snaked down the lobby. Its huge, greedy fingers were aimed right at the Grimms and Puck.

Sabrina did the only thing she could think of. She dragged her family past the security guard and into the waiting elevator at the end of the hall. She scanned the dozens of buttons and found the one she wanted—OBSERVATION DECK. Then the doors closed and the elevator started to rise.

"You know, I lived in this city for years and I've never been to the top," Puck said. "I hope the souvenir shop is still open."

The elevator came to a stop. When the door opened, a blast of cold air and snow hit their faces. Through it they could just see the outline of a hot-air balloon, tangled on top of the building.

Oz was frantically trying to unfasten several ropes that had caught on the building's spire. The basket swayed dangerously in the wind, dumping some of its contents onto the roof of the building.

"Turn the witch off!" Sabrina shouted.

Oz looked down and snarled.

"Mr. Diggs, someone is going to get hurt," Granny added. "That is, if they haven't already."

"You fools!" Oz shouted from his basket. "What do I care if a bunch of humans die? The master has promised me that I will rule over them all. A few lives mean nothing to me."

Sabrina looked over the edge of the building. The witch had begun to climb the facade, digging her huge hands into the building's concrete frame. It reminded Sabrina of a movie she had seen once.

"Oz, you told me you were my mother's best friend," she called out to the Wizard. "She trusted you. Regardless of your plans I don't think you wanted to hurt her."

"I didn't. He told me he had a big plan for your parents. He said they'd give birth to a future where Everafters ruled the world."

Sabrina glanced down again. The witch was now only a dozen floors away from them. Oz paid no attention. He continued to cut his ropes one by one.

Puck's wings popped out of his back and flapped fiercely. "If you try to fly away from here I will blast a hole in your little balloon. I swear it."

If Oz was worried by the threat, it didn't stop him. He cut the last rope and then waved good-bye. In a flash, Sabrina did something she never would have guessed she had the courage to do. She grabbed the loose rope.

Her brain told her to let go, in fact it was begging her to, but she refused, even as she soared higher and higher into the air. She knew what she was doing was insane. She might die, but the alternative was worse. She couldn't live knowing she'd let her parents' kidnapper get away.

"Let go, you foolish child!" Oz shouted from above. Sabrina could see he was struggling to untie the rope she was holding onto, but he was having no success.

"How do I wake them up?" Sabrina cried, pulling herself hand over hand up the rope. "How do I wake up my parents?"

"This is all pointless, Sabrina. You can't fight the master or me. The future is coming. Now let go."

"No!" Sabrina had reached the basket. She grabbed onto the side.

The Wizard's face filled with sorrow. "Then I'm sorry, Sabrina." He pushed her hard and she lost her grip. She snatched at his hand but grabbed something small and silver instead. The remote control. Wind filled her ears like a lion's roar and she could feel gravity pulling her toward the ground.

10

abrina!"

She heard someone shouting her name over the wind. "Sabrina. I've got you!"

And then, she wasn't falling anymore. She rubbed the coldness out of her eyes. Puck had her in his arms and was grinning at her as he flew them back up to the top of the building. The robot witch was there, now practically on top of Relda and Daphne. Panicked, Sabrina pointed the little silver controller at the monster and pushed at the dozen buttons. Just as the robot was about to squash her family, it froze.

Puck touched down next to Granny and Daphne. The little girl was in hysterics and hugged Sabrina tighter than she ever had. Granny joined the hug.

"Come on, people!" Puck said. "Did you really think I was going to let you die?"

Daphne pulled away from Sabrina for a moment. She sniffled and then held out something to her sister. "This fell out of the balloon." It was their mother's journal. Sabrina took it and opened it. In the back was the yellowing paper. Veronica's speech was still inside.

By the light of the witch's still glowing eye, Granny Relda took the speech and quickly read it to herself. A proud smile spread across her face. She handed it back to Sabrina. "I think the Everafters should hear this."

"I could give it to Puck. He could read it to them."

"*Liebling,* these are your mother's words."

Sabrina met her grandmother's gaze, lifted her chin, and nodded. "OK. We need to get everyone together. Puck, how do we turn this building bright purple?"

Daphne looked at the witch. "Granny, we're going to need an awful lot of forgetful dust," the little girl said.

• • •

Sabrina sat in a back room at the Golden Egg. Daphne sat behind her with a brush combing her long blond hair while Sabrina studied her mother's writing. She fretted over every syllable and comma, hoping that she could somehow do the speech justice. She was not one for speeches, especially in front of Everafters.

"Don't be afraid," Daphne said. "I'll be standing right next to you."

"Good," Sabrina answered. "You can deflect the pies and rotten tomatoes they toss at me."

"I think that only happens in cartoons," Daphne replied. "Still, I'll keep an eye out for them."

The door opened and Mustardseed appeared. He smiled and gave the girls a wink. "They are ready for you."

"We're coming," Daphne said, and Mustardseed gestured that he'd wait in the hall.

"Do I really have to do this?" Sabrina said. "What if I screw it up? What if I ruin what Mom was trying to do?"

"You won't," Daphne said as she pulled her sister to her feet. "And even if you do, your hair looks fabulous."

"Thanks."

"For a jerkazoid," Daphne added with a smile.

They joined Mustardseed in the hallway. He led them into the restaurant, where they found Puck, addressing the crowd. He was wearing a jeweled crown, an oversized purple robe, and carrying an enormous scepter. He strolled back and forth trying to seem dignified while struggling with his outfit.

"Attention!" he shouted. "There has been a great upheaval in the last few days. My father, your leader, lies dead. I have returned to the kingdom to rule."

"Get on with it, Puck!" one of the dwarfs shouted. "We lost patience with you nearly half an hour ago."

Puck sneered and gestured to Sabrina and Daphne. The girls stepped onto the stage and stared at the crowd.

"Now, I know they are terribly ugly and difficult to look at," Puck said, causing Sabrina to growl. "But these girls have got something to say. When they are done, you fools can go back to fighting if you want."

He turned to Sabrina and frowned. "Good luck," he said. "They're a disrespectful bunch."

Sabrina looked down at the speech. "This was written by my mother," she said.

"We can't hear you!" someone shouted.

"Speak up!"

Sabrina looked to her sister for help.

"You may not talk a lot but you've never had a problem with volume," Daphne said.

Sabrina cleared her throat and started again. "This was written by my mother on the eve of her disappearance almost two years ago."

Suddenly, the crowd was silent. "I'm afraid that I will probably never be the speaker my mother was but I will read it word for word. It outlines her ideas for you. I hope it helps."

Sabrina looked at her mother's writing, studying the curves of her letters, trying to understand the mind that wrote the words.

"I will not stand here and claim to know your hearts. You have had difficult lives. You've seen dreams ripped apart. You've watched as suffering came to you like floodwaters. I am human. I am blessed. I live in a world that believes in me. Your very existence defies what humanity can accept. You are supposed to be bedtime stories—not flesh and blood. Thus, you have had to live in the shadows, accepting the table scraps you could find and yearning for the life humans take for granted.

"It doesn't have to be like this. You are few, but together you are many. Combining your talents, working for one another's benefit, lifting one another up when you fall—this is the path to your happiness. If you could work together as a community, you could build empires with your small numbers, but instead you have chosen to squabble and divide. Well, I say it's time to put hatred aside and hold your brothers' and sisters' hands. You don't need humanity to believe in you. You only need to believe in each other."

Sabrina continued reading. She did her best to make eye contact with those in the crowd and she held Daphne's hand for support. She could feel her mother's thoughts inside her, how Veronica felt about every word she had put in the speech. Veronica described a world that Everafters could embrace, a world where they could work together, for the benefit of one another. It was a simple plan based on common sense and a common purpose. She described a government where majority ruled the day but a passionate minority could not be trampled. She recommended that leaders be elected rather than born. She talked of schools and hospitals. She spoke of science and technologies helping them keep pace with the modern world, but mostly she spoke of finding common ground.

"You are all Everafters," Sabrina concluded. "Your neighbor's needs are your needs. His passions are your passions, and his heartbreak is your sorrow as well. If you can treat his struggles as your own, you will celebrate your successes together. It doesn't matter that he may be feathered or furry. It makes no difference if he is on two legs or twenty. Don't waste time finding differences. When you talk to your neighbors, close your eyes and you will truly see them."

After she spoke the last words, she thanked them and stood back, wondering if they would choose her mother's ideals over their own isolation and squabbling. For a long moment there was silence. Sabrina looked to Puck and Daphne and Granny Relda, but they were as trapped in the moment as she.

And then Mother Goose stood up. "Thank you, Sabrina Grimm, daughter of Veronica. You have served your family well," she said, and she began to clap. Others joined her, and soon the entire audience was on its feet clapping: Yahoos, dwarfs, pirates, fairies, and goblins alike. Moments later, a familiar chant began.

"Grimm! Grimm! Grimm!"

Tears ran down Sabrina's cheeks. They weren't tears of sadness but of great pride. Their mother had tried to build something important. For Sabrina, it was the first time since discovering her family history that she truly understood it. Being a Grimm wasn't just being a fairy-tale detective. It was being the person who helps when no one else will lend a hand. Being a Grimm was something to be proud of, not something to run from.

Granny Relda pulled the girls close to her.

"I'm ready to be part of this family," Sabrina said.

"I never had any doubts, child," the old woman said as a tear rolled down her cheek. "I never had any doubts."

Daphne hugged her sister tightly. "I'm glad you're back. I can't do this without you."

• • •

The family found their car parked under three feet of snow. Mustardseed blasted it with a little fire and it was clean and clear in no time. Mr. Canis got in awkwardly. He was still seven feet tall and found it difficult to get behind the wheel. He started the car's engine and allowed it to warm up.

Hamstead stood nearby. He hadn't spoken to anyone since Mr. Canis had found him sitting in his darkened hotel room. Now he shuffled his feet and looked down at the pavement. Sabrina understood. His broken heart had crushed his spirit. Sabrina was brokenhearted, too, though she was working hard to hide it. Not only was Puck not coming back to Ferryport Landing with them, he hadn't come to say good-bye.

"You've given us some hope for the future," Mustardseed said to her.

"Good luck," Sabrina said. "And don't let your brother ruin everything. If he has his way he'll turn the city into a junkyard he can play in all day."

"Yes, I remember him suggesting just that," Mustardseed said. "Don't worry. The Trickster King has other plans."

"Well, we better get home and find out how to wake up your mom and dad," Granny said to the girls. "And the two of you need to start your training."

"Training? What have we been doing all this time?" Sabrina asked.

"Following me around and getting in trouble," the old woman said. "Now that you both are ready and willing, we're going to explore what's inside the Hall of Wonders. You girls are going to learn to be proper fairy-tale detectives."

Granny Relda and the girls got into the car. Hamstead followed, and they all rolled down their windows and waved goodbye to Mustardseed. Mr. Canis pulled away from the curb to a symphony of backfires and rattles, and pointed the car in the direction of Ferryport Landing. Sabrina watched out the window as the city rolled by. She spotted her father's favorite movie theater and the place her mother loved to buy secondhand books. Someday she'd come back here, but there was no hurry. She had a new place to call home.

Suddenly, there was a rapping sound on the roof of the car. Sabrina craned her neck but couldn't see anything. Another pounding occurred and then a fiery blast raced past the car. The fire streaked high into the air and then came down in front of the automobile. Canis slammed on the brakes. Sabrina watched it all, slowly realizing that the blast was attached to a person, a woman in fact, who came down from the sky wearing what appeared to be a rocket pack strapped on her back.

"Bess!" Mr. Hamstead cried.

"Ernie!"

Mr. Hamstead looked bewildered. He leaped out of the car and everyone followed.

"Don't go, Ernie!" Bess cried.

"Bess, what are you doing here?"

"I came to stop you. I love you. I don't care about your secret. It doesn't matter to me that you're a pig," the woman cried, rushing to Mr. Hamstead and taking his hand.

"Bess, I don't know what to say," the man said, fumbling for words.

"Say you love me, too."

"I do love you," Mr. Hamstead said. "But we're too different. It would never work."

"Not so fast," Bess said. She took a step back and suddenly her body went through an amazing transformation. It was an incredible sight, not unlike the one that Hamstead went through each time he became a pig; only Bess became something quite different. She was a cow.

"So you're one of the Three Little Pigs, huh?" Bess said. "Allow me to introduce myself. I'm the Cow That Jumped Over the Moon."

Daphne's hand quickly went into her mouth as Bess lifted off the ground.

Hamstead grinned from ear to ear and clapped wildly. "I love you, baby!" he cried.

Bess drifted down to the pavement and morphed back into

her human form. She rushed to Hamstead's side. "Stay with me," she begged.

Hamstead turned to Granny Relda with hopeful eyes. "I'll miss you, Relda," he said, hugging the old woman. "But I love her. I can't leave."

"I couldn't be happier for you," Granny said. "Ferryport Landing won't be the same without you, Ernest."

"So where are you crazy kids going on your honeymoon?" Daphne said, wrapping her arms around Hamstead's generous middle.

Everyone laughed.

"I'm thinking Hawaii," Bess said, causing Hamstead's face to spontaneously morph into his pig form.

"Or Paris," he oinked, then pulled himself together. "There's a lot to see and I've got a bit of cabin fever, if you know what I mean."

He turned to Mr. Canis. "Take care of yourself, Wolf."

Canis nodded and shook Hamstead's hand. "It has been an honor, Pig."

As the group celebrated, Hamstead pulled Sabrina and Daphne aside. "Girls, I fear that things are not going well with our old friend Canis."

Sabrina nodded. "I thought I was the only one who noticed."

"Your grandmother has always had a lot of faith in his ability to keep the Wolf at bay, but I don't believe that is always going to be the case," he said as he removed a chain from around his neck. There was a small silver key attached to it. He slipped it over Daphne's head and urged her to hide it under her shirt.

"What's this?" the little girl asked.

"It's your plan B. It opens a safety deposit box. You'll find a weapon inside . . . something so powerful it can stop even the Wolf. Mr. Boarman and Mr. Swineheart can help you use it if things get bad. Don't let it fall into the wrong hands and don't tell anyone you have it. It would be devastating."

"I'll give this to Granny," Daphne said, patting the key.

"No," Hamstead whispered. "Don't tell her anything."

"But—"

"Just trust me."

Sabrina, Daphne, Granny Relda, and Mr. Canis said their good-byes to Mr. Hamstead and Bess. They got into the car, gave a farewell honk, and then drove away.

Sabrina settled into her seat and realized she was feeling depressed. When they'd heard that thump on the roof of the car, she'd thought for a moment it was Puck.

Daphne looked at her sister and seemed to read her mind. "You know, I really can't believe Puck. What a jerkazoid," she said. "So what if he's a king. He's going to be lousy at it! He should have come back to Ferryport Landing."

"What do I care," Sabrina said, trying to hide her feelings. "I say, 'good riddance.'"

Daphne turned and gazed out the back window, then let out a startled laugh. She nudged Sabrina to take a look as well. Sabrina turned in her seat and was shocked by what she saw. Following not far behind them was the six-story mechanical Wicked Witch of the West. Perched on the top of its hat was Puck. He had pink insect wings coming out of his back and he held the little silver remote in his hands.

"What's that stuff he spray-painted on the robot?" Daphne said.

Sabrina smiled. "It says, 'Ferryport Landing or Bust!'"

"Is he following us home?" Daphne cried.

Granny turned in her seat and smiled. "I believe he is, *liebling*."

"And he's bringing his toy with him," Mr. Canis grumbled.

"I think we're going to need an awful lot of forgetful dust," Sabrina said.

To be continued in

THE SISTERS GRIMM

BOOK FIVE
MAGIC AND OTHER
MISDEMEANORS

ABOUT THE AUTHOR

Michael Buckley is the *New York Times* bestselling author of the *Sisters Grimm* series. He has also written and developed television shows for many networks. *The Mole People* and *The New Sideshow* can be seen regularly on the Discovery Channel. Michael lives in New York City.

This book was designed by Jay Colvin and art-directed by Chad W. Beckerman. It is set in Adobe Garamond, a typeface that is based on those created in the sixteenth century by Claude Garamond. Garamond modeled his typefaces on those created by Venetian printers at the end of the fifteenth century. The modern version used in this book was designed by Robert Slimbach, who studied Garamond's historic typefaces at the Plantin-Moretus Museum in Antwerp, Belgium.

The capital letters at the beginning of each chapter are set in Daylilies, designed by Judith Sutcliffe. She created the typeface by decorating Goudy Old Style capitals with lilies.